JUNIOR
HERO BLUES

J·K· PENDRAGON

TRITON
BOOKS

Triton Books
PO Box 1537
Burnsville, NC 28714
www.tritonya.com
Triton Books is an imprint of Riptide Publishing.
www.RiptidePublishing.com

Junior Hero Blues

Cover art: Michelle Fairbanks, mfairbanks.carbonmade.com
Editors: Rachel Haimowitz, May Peterson
Layout: L.C. Chase, lcchase.com/design.htm

ISBN: 978-1-62649-456-5

First edition
November, 2016

Also available in ebook:
ISBN: 978-1-62649-455-8

JUNIOR
HERO BLUES

J.K. PENDRAGON

To all the gay superheroes out there. You know who you are!

table of
CONTENTS

PART ONE

CHAPTER ONE

When I woke up, my mask was lying beside me on the ground, and I felt like my entire head had been squeezed like a pimple.

It took me a few minutes to get my bearings, and by the time I realized that the Raven was there with me, she was putting my mask back over my eyes and checking my vitals. Masks have a way of obscuring expressions, but I could see that her jaw was tight and her lips were even thinner than usual.

"What happened?" I groaned, my voice raspy. I was starting to get memories back, of the smoke and explosions of the battle, and of *him*. That bastard smashing my head into a mirror—I raised a hand to my forehead and felt crusted blood through my glove—and then of us fighting, and of a rather unheroic rage that had come over me as we did so. The last thing I remembered was my hands on either side of his head, shooting sonic waves into his ears so hard that his eyes were rolling back, and his big meaty hands around my neck, squeezing me into darkness.

"Don't know." The Raven's ambiguously Slavic accent was harsher than normal. "I found you here, with your mask off. Who did it, do you know?"

"Yeah." I coughed. "Who do you think? Jimmy Black."

I guess I should back up a bit. Jimmy Black was my sworn enemy, if you go for dramatics like that (I totally do), and I'd met him a few months before, when all this crap with the Organization started. I'd been on a date with Rick Rykov. My first date. Ever, that is, and I was pretty convinced that the whole thing was a setup to make fun of me, because that would just be typical. But then Rick actually showed up at the café and we sat there for twenty minutes drinking coffee and discussing our lives like regular people, and there was absolutely no sign of the whole thing being a prank or some plan concocted by him and his friends to humiliate me.

I mean, aside from being gay, Rick was, like, standard bully material. He was a football player, even—six feet of lean teenage muscle and popularity. And I have a theory that being gay in high school just pushes your social standing to an extreme either way. Like, if you're already popular and then you come out as gay, you become like this amazing, brave individual who inspires change (exhibit A: Rick Rykov). But if you come out as gay, and you're that weird little Spanish dude who came to America in first grade and couldn't speak any English, who decided to compensate for that fact by eating a bug in front of his entire class, which was never forgotten, ever, by anyone . . .

Well, see exhibit B: Javier Medina (that's me, by the way). Skinny, brown, nerdy. I'm sure you can picture it. That, combined with my family not exactly being wealthy, meant I got picked on a lot in school, even before the bug thing, so I'm a little skittish. Or possibly a lot skittish. You decide.

So anyway, naturally, considering my rather extensive history with bullies, when a super hot, super popular football player came striding down the hall toward me after class one day, my first instinct was to run away. Unfortunately, Kendall (who apparently has superhearing that I don't know about) had overheard that Rick was planning on asking me out, and grabbed my arm to keep me from escaping. She's pretty heavyset, and I guess she was using her weight to her advantage, because I was basically rooted to the spot despite having, you know, moderate superstrength.

So then Rick strolled up, cool as you please, and *introduced himself*. Like, he full-on shook my hand. As if it was a job interview. And then he asked me out, and I was thinking that I might be stupid enough to eat a bug, but I sure as hell wasn't stupid enough to think that Rick Rykov was actually asking me out on a date. So I told him to eff off.

Yeah right. I actually said something along the lines of, "Uhhhh . . . you want to go . . . on a date? With me? Wh-hyy?"

And he said, "Because I like you. I think you're cute, so I thought we could get to know each other a bit better, over coffee."

At this point I was basically giving myself whiplash looking around trying to see if I was in the process of being ambushed with the eventual intent to stick my head in the toilet. And then I got kind of angry because, like, here I was, busting my butt every single day to save people's lives and keep the public safe—screw putting up with this high school bullying crap.

So I decided I would go out with Rick, and if he or any of his buff football friends decided to try to pull one over me, I was just going to spontaneously snap and beat the crap out of them (or at least use my powers to pull some fun tricks with them) and plead temporary insanity to Captain Liberty after the fact.

Rick seemed pleased, and a little surprised that I'd agreed. We set a date, and I went in fully expecting to be doused with whipped cream, or laughed and jeered at, or at the very least stood up.

But Rick was there, leaning back in one of the little spindly café chairs that looked like it might break under his weight, and sipping some frothy drink. When I sat down, he shook my hand again, and then we just sort of . . . started talking.

Which I know isn't a big deal, because, like, people talk all the time. But not me. I mean, I talk to Kendall, because she's my best friend and has been forever and we tell each other everything. I talk to my parents, in Spanish mostly, which is still a bit easier for me, funnily enough (although I'm sure you can tell I have an absolutely superb grasp of the English language). But with everyone else? It's kind of like the fewer syllables I can use, the better. I mumble my way through life. I just can't make myself say what I'm thinking most of the time.

So yeah, it was pleasantly surprising to be able to talk to Rick. He asked me questions, and waited patiently while I answered them, and then offered information about himself. He lived with his parents in a really nice part of town, although pretty close to me, and had a sister and a cat. And I told him, a bit defensively, that I lived with my parents in a crappy little apartment that didn't allow pets, and that my dad worked on computers and my mom worked at a gas station so we could have a little extra income. I was all set for Rick to be all judgey or awkward (or worse, feel bad for me) about my poorness, but he didn't seem to care about that at all. He actually seemed to genuinely want to get to know me.

And then, just when I was starting to relax and believe that this was actually a thing that was happening and I wasn't going to, you know, die, Rick's phone rang. He had a sort of awkward conversation and said, looking really let down, "I'm sorry, I've got to go to work. Last-minute thing." Then his face brightened up a bit. "But we should do this again sometime."

I agreed, and he went off, and I was left sitting there for about ten minutes finishing my coffee and thinking. And then my phone rang too.

I should have figured it out right then and there.

It was the Legion dispatch, about as polite as ever, which is to say one step up from a robot. Actually, scratch that, the Legion AI was way friendlier.

So she was all like, "There's an incident downtown, not far from your location. Can you respond?"

And I figured why not, since I was pretty pumped at that moment, and anyway, it was my job. Like, I got paid for it and everything. So I told her I'd be there in like two minutes, and grabbed my bag and headed out.

Now, listen up, because I'm going to let you in on a little secret about switching from your civilian clothes into your superhero getup.

The telephone booth thing?

Utter bull-crap.

I mean, maybe except for old pros like Captain Liberty. I've seen him change into his costume so fast it was like he must have been wearing a tear-away outfit, complete with, like, origami cape and boots in his back pocket. But for the rest of us, it's three-plus minutes of awkwardly hunching on top of a building—try even finding a telephone booth these days—ripping off your clothes and pulling on the parts of your costume that don't fit under them, and then you have to try to fit everything, including your shoes, into your backpack. And *then* you have to look for a place to stash your backpack where it won't be stolen or, like, crapped on by pigeons or something.

And the Legion really does expect you to respond to a call within like five minutes. I don't know why they haven't invented some sort of quick-change technology. Maybe they have, and they just don't make it available to Junior Heroes.

It's a complete rip-off being a Junior Hero, by the way. You're supposed to be only assigned to low-risk stuff, but half the time it's just as dangerous as anything else anyway, and the rest of the time it's freaking boring. You don't get any of the cool gadgets, and there are all these rules . . .

Anyway, I guess I should skip ahead to the action.

I hadn't really been given any info by dispatch besides that the incident was a jewelry store break-in, and when I arrived, the alarm was going off already, so that meant the police were on their way. But of course by the time they got here, it probably would have been too late. It was up to me to stop the thieves (if they hadn't already finished up and left in the time it had taken me to find my mask in the bottom of my backpack), so I jumped down outside the glass doorway and warned all the civilians to take cover, before heading on in.

The thieves were still here, but it looked like they were getting ready to leave. My first clue that something was up was the fact that none of them were holding any loot, besides the head guy, and all he had was a briefcase. The second thing was that they weren't wearing normal robber attire (not that robbers have a uniform but, you know) and instead they were wearing dark-colored skintight suits that looked a lot like Legion costumes only . . . well, darker. Also, they all had on masks, but not your old-fashioned balaclava-type masks. No, these were molded ones, heavy-duty, doubling-as-face-armor-type masks, like only heroes wear. Well, heroes and villains.

That confirmed my suspicions: these guys were with the Organization. I reached for my watch and subtly tapped the panic button that alerted the Legion that I needed backup. In the meantime, I knew it was up to me to either stop them, or else stall them until some more powerful Legion members could arrive and take them out.

All this happened in about five seconds, of course. Basically I walked in, the tinkly bell on the door went off, the guys inside looked at me, and I pressed the button on my watch. And then the guy with the briefcase turned around and distracted me with his junk.

Okay, you have to cut me some slack here, because one, I am a hormonal teenager, and two, it was, like, *right there*, and, um, big. And it's not like I'm not used to seeing guys in spandex and/or spandex-like materials, seeing as I belong to the Legion and everything, but jeez, this guy was really impressive. It was almost obscene.

So at that moment I had about two thoughts in my mind, one of which was *Distract them until backup arrives!* and the other of which was *Holy crap, his bulge,* so my first instinct was to distract him by pointing out his penis to him.

I know. Shut up.

"What the hell is *that*?" I gestured dramatically at his crotch. "That's not appropriate for children!"

The guy just stared at me, and I'm pretty sure his expression was something like incredulous, although it was hard to tell because, you know, mask. His eyes flickered over me though, and I remembered belatedly that as a superhero in a midriff-baring costume, I was not exactly above the "not appropriate for children" criticism. Also, the way he was looking at me was . . . I don't know, kind of sexy but in a way that made me feel a bit uncomfortable and squirmy. And angry too.

"Hey!" I said loudly. "I'm talking to you!"

The guy shrugged, seeming a lot more relaxed than his two cronies, and grinned at me. "What's the problem? I have nothing to hide."

"Oh yeah?" I flushed under my mask. "Then why are you hiding your *face*?"

I'm sorry, by the way.

If you went into this thinking that it was a story about one of those epic, always cool heroes with the witty one-liners, who only pretends to be shy and dorky for the sake of his alter ego, you've probably realized by now that that is not what you're getting. I, Javier Medina—or Blue Spark, as I'm known to the citizens of Liberty City—am one-hundred-percent dork, through and through. The mask only makes it worse. So yeah, I apologize. If this isn't what you're into, I'd recommend Captain Liberty's autobiography. Not the current Captain Liberty, though, I'm pretty sure he's super boring. But the Captain Liberty in the forties was pretty cool and witty.

Except that he was kind of a huge raging misogynist. Kendall's all into the feminist history of superheroes, so I know these things.

What was I talking about? Oh yeah, I was detailing my epic levels of fail.

Well, let's get on with that, then.

So the guy took a step toward me, and then another. And then he was staring down at me with this dark, evil glint in his eyes, and smiling like a crocodile. "Listen, kid, if you knew what you were dealing with, you'd get the hell out of the way."

"I know what you are," I said, pretty bravely in my opinion, considering that the guy was like three times my size. "You're with the Organization, aren't you? What's your name, Evil McBigDick?"

I was stalling here, just so you know. I'm usually a lot more to the point. I think.

Anyway, I must have struck a nerve, because the guy's smile went away, and he made a little signal to his cronies with his fingers. Then he said, "It's Jimmy," and brought his fist up into my stomach, catapulting me into the air and through the glass display window. "Jimmy Black."

Stupid name for a supervillain, if you ask me.

So I went flying through the glass and it shattered all around me, and there I was lying on the pavement, staring up at the tall buildings and the sky. My stomach hurt pretty bad, and I was trying hard to breathe, and little bits of glass were digging into the bare skin on my back. I know, I know, midriff-baring costume, really, really stupid. But it shows off my abs, and my cool markings (more on those later), and I don't think it's fair that only the girl superheroes get to look sexy while fighting crime. Plus it's not like the rest of my uniform is super heavy-duty. The thing about me is, I'm generally fast enough to get out of the way before taking any blows. And if Jimmy hadn't been distracting me with his junk, I would have been able to. Okay, that's probably enough about his junk.

The minute I could actually take half of a proper breath, I sat up to see that my backup had arrived, finally. Two superheroes—I think I recognized Lady Deathquake (awesome name) and Wolfhound— were locked in battle with two of Jimmy's cronies. But Jimmy himself, not to mention the briefcase of whatever he'd been in the process of stealing, was nowhere to be seen.

Then I spotted him: running down the sidewalk, shoving pedestrians out of the way as he went, and turning down an alleyway. There was no time to alert the other heroes, or call for more backup. I had to follow him.

I used my powers for the first time that day, catapulting myself off the ground with waves of sound that sent the broken window glass scattering. I bounced over the heads of the crowd, hit the ground hard, and screeched to a halt next to the alley that Jimmy had turned down. For a moment I didn't see him, but then I looked up and saw a dark figure running up the sand-colored wall like it was horizontal.

Great, just great. I should mention at this point that I sort of have this issue with heights. I've had it all my life, but getting electrocuted and falling off a tower a year earlier probably hadn't helped. The thing about my powers is, I can use them to fly . . . sort of. I can basically generate sound waves from certain spots on my body, mainly my palms and feet. If I shoot out wave after wave, I can propel myself through the air, or else do this stupid little hop to stay in one place.

I'm serious, it looks really ridiculous.

And I think that if I could, like, actually fly, my fear of heights wouldn't be as bad, because I'd obviously never have to worry about falling. As it is, "flying" for me is pretty much constant jumping and falling, and the worst case of stomach butterflies anyone's ever experienced. I deserve a medal for what I go through.

So anyway, there was Jimmy running up the wall sideways (what kind of freaking power is that?) and about to disappear onto the roof, stolen briefcase still in hand. I shouted at him, something like, "Hey, Jimmy BigDick!" hoping he'd slow down or turn around or be so surprised that he fell off the wall or something. But he just kept running, so I had no choice but to catapult myself up into the air, and do my stupid little bounce thing to catch up with him. At least no one was watching.

He jumped onto the top of the roof, and I came up over the edge and twisted in the air so that I was horizontal, and shot toward his back, slamming us both down. The roof was one of those stupid ones that are covered in gravel, and it burned my knees (although I will admit my costume does a pretty good job of protecting me, despite being lightweight—it's some sort of secret Legion material).

Jimmy swore and rolled over to throw another punch into my gut, but I was too fast for him this time. I dodged out of the way and ripped the briefcase from his hand, and then he spun on the ground, surprisingly agile for such a big guy, and knocked my feet out from under me—which, rude—and I fell, shocked enough to lose my grip on the briefcase.

He grabbed it in midair, flung it over the other side of the building, and ran after it, catching it as he went over. I stood up and raced after him, angry enough to jump off the edge of a building without freaking out and stalling, for once.

He was running down the side of the building, and I was falling, but luckily I managed to fall right on top of him. I landed my feet directly on his shoulders and kicked hard, shoving him off the wall. He fell, face-first and grasping at thin air, and I twisted and sent out shock waves just in time to stop myself from hitting the ground. I made a bit of a crater in the asphalt, though, which was less than optimal, even if it did look cool. The Legion frowns on destruction of city property. Obviously the glass window wasn't my fault, but the crater sort of totally was. Oh well, maybe they wouldn't notice.

Jimmy had created some damage himself, cracking the asphalt and putting a decent-sized dent in a manhole with his head. For a moment I thought he was out, but when I took a step toward him, he groaned and lifted himself up onto his knees, glaring at me with a look of seething hatred. I almost took a step back, I was so shocked by the intensity of his expression, but part of me was pleased too that I'd actually gotten him angry.

I kept walking toward him, nervous that this wasn't over, but also relieved by the fact that he seemed to be having trouble getting back onto his feet. I wasn't sure what I was supposed to do now, since we're provided with handcuffs to incapacitate petty crooks, but based on the fact that this guy had just survived a ten-story fall and lived to tell the tale, I suspected they weren't going to work on him.

There were civilians around too, gasping and screaming and pulling out their phones. All that stupid stuff that civilians do when they should be running for their lives. Sometimes I think that the Legion is so sensationalized people forget that what we do is actually dangerous, and that, you know, civilian casualties are a thing that happens.

Jimmy was still glaring up at me, his face sharp and angry, and then he glanced down for a second, and I saw that he was looking at the briefcase, which had fallen directly between us. I lunged for it, but he got there first. He grabbed it, and I went to tackle him, but he dropped out from under me. The manhole cover skidded across the cracked asphalt, and I landed over the open hole.

The crowd around us gasped, and, trying not to think about what this meant, I jumped down after him.

I landed in, you guessed it, sewage.

Eww.

I propelled myself back up out of it, but not before it had pretty much soaked me through. It smelled like . . . well, I'm not going to describe how it smelled, because I don't want to relive it, and I'm sure you can put your imagination to the task.

So there I was, bouncing up and down in the air and dripping sewage. I had always imagined that sewers were pretty small, but this one was huge. I'd fallen at least thirty feet, and the light from the manhole above did almost nothing to illuminate my surroundings. I tried to make my markings glow brighter, which they tend to do anyway when I'm upset or embarrassed or *pissed off*, but they didn't help at all. I couldn't hear anything either, besides a bunch of useless splashing echoes. I had no idea which way Jimmy had gone, or even which way the exits were.

For a moment I was completely stuck, and then I remembered that I have sound powers that are good for stuff besides destroying city property, and closed my eyes. I brought my hands up, and shot out little waves of sound, listening as they bounced back to me, revealing archways and tunnels in all directions, and down one, the water rippling as if someone was running atop it.

I lunged after him, nearly dousing myself again. I heard him gasp and swear as he realized that I was still following him, and again felt super smug at having managed to get a reaction out of him. I was mostly flying blind at this point, since I wasn't staying still long enough for any echoes to get back to me, but I could hear him ahead of me. Footsteps on the wall, and then the sound of a manhole being wrenched open. I shot upward toward the blinding light, and saw his backlit figure disappearing through the hole.

I emerged out onto the street, ignoring the screams from the inevitable crowd, and squinted around to see where he had gone, but no matter where I looked, there was no Jimmy, and no briefcase. And there I was, panting, soaking wet, my body starting to throb in pain, and absolutely nothing to show for my efforts.

Oh, and I smelled like crap.

The rest of the day pretty much sucked. Lady Deathquake and the Wolfhound were mad at me for going after Jimmy myself instead of alerting a Senior Hero, I was mad at me for losing him, and everyone was giving me a wide berth due to the fact that I was soaking wet and fuming.

Lady Deathquake and Wolfhound took me to the Legion headquarters in their car—although Wolfhound put a towel on the seat first—and then we all went up the elevator and into a conference room, where I was surprised, and not at all happy, to see Captain Liberty himself.

"What are you doing here?" I blurted.

The captain raised his eyebrows at me. He wasn't wearing a mask, since he didn't bother with a secret identity. Everyone knew that he was Dr. Paulo Flores, a Filipino-American professor at Liberty City University, a certified doctor of medicine and two other sciences, as well as Captain Liberty, the elected head of the Legion of Liberty. He was also really, really hot for an older guy.

And I was standing in front of him, smelling like a public toilet.

"Where else would I be?" He smiled calmly. "I'm here to conduct a debriefing of the situation that occurred today."

"Yeah, but it was just a jewelry-store robbery." I swallowed. "Wasn't it?"

"I think you already know better than that, Blue," said the captain disapprovingly. "I don't imagine you'd have called for backup otherwise."

"They were Organization," said Wolfhound. "No doubt about it. Though why they were robbing a jewelry store, I have no idea."

"There was a briefcase," I said. "The leader, he said his name was Jimmy Black, he got away with it."

"Mmm." Captain Liberty pursed his lips. "The jewelry store was in fact a front for one of our undercover operations."

I gaped at him. "Then why did you send me there alone?"

"It was an oversight," said Captain Liberty. "I'll be looking into our dispatch procedures shortly."

"Good," I said petulantly, and Captain Liberty gave me a look that made me feel like he was my mother and I was *el niño malcriado.* I shut up.

"Any idea what was in the briefcase, then?" asked Lady Deathquake.

Captain Liberty nodded. "Possibly. But I don't want to speculate until I have more information. I'll expect detailed reports from all of you by email no later than midnight."

Great. Homework.

"For now," continued Captain Liberty, "you can all return home for the day. Blue, you may want to change. Do you have a set of clothes here?"

I sighed. "Yeah. Do you think I could get my costume cleaned?"

"Of course." Captain Liberty smiled at me again. "I'll see to it immediately."

So that was how I found myself sitting on one of the comfy chairs outside Captain Liberty's office, wearing some old baggy street clothes that I'd left at the headquarters for emergencies, and playing Pong on my phone. I guess my disguise really does work pretty well, because the Wolfhound walked right past me into Captain Liberty's office at one point, and shut the door before announcing, "There's a Mexican sitting outside your office."

Superhearing can be a bit of a curse sometimes.

"He's Spanish, not Mexican." Captain Liberty's voice was so quiet that I suspected he knew I could hear him through the wall. "Though I don't believe that is any of your business either way. What can I do for you, Frank?"

"You can explain to me what all this is about," grumbled Wolfhound. "Since when does the Legion keep secrets from its members?"

"I'm not keeping secrets," replied Captain Liberty. "I'm merely avoiding the spread of disinformation. Believe me, when I know for certain what's going on, everyone in the Legion will be made aware."

I lost my game of Pong and exited the app before a new one could start. A lady in heels and a tight pencil skirt walked past me, and I shrunk deeper into the chair, hoping she didn't notice that I was eavesdropping.

"I know you've got suspicions," said the Wolfhound. "What was at that jewelry store?"

"Various things." Captain Liberty was silent for a bit. "The one that's chief among my concerns? One part of a data package that could potentially be used against the Legion if reconciled with the other parts."

"Used against us in what way?"

Captain Liberty didn't respond.

"It's those damn chips, isn't it?" growled Wolfhound. "They're bad news. The old Captain Liberty would never—"

"The decision to implement the chips was based on a majority vote."

"Yeah, but you encouraged it." Silence again. "I'm telling people."

"That's what I was going to do," said Captain Liberty, "as soon as it's confirmed that is the data which was stolen."

"You'd better."

Captain Liberty sounded annoyed. "Frank, I am a very busy man. Is there anything else you'd like to discuss with me?"

"No, I think that's enough."

The door slammed open, and I shoved my phone back up to my face as Wolfhound stormed past me with a growl. The door stayed open, and after a moment, I heard Captain Liberty stand and come to the door. I kept my phone at eye-height and glanced over as he leaned around the door to look at me.

"Javier." His voice was calm, but I was absolutely certain that he was about to tell me off for eavesdropping. "Why don't you come into my office for a minute? Shut the door behind you."

I got up and shoved my phone into my pocket, trying to think of an excuse as I followed him into his office. I hadn't meant to be eavesdropping! He should know better than to conduct private conversations with someone outside who had superhearing. Right?

Captain Liberty sighed and reached up to remove his cape. He hung it on his special cape hanger next to his desk and sat down, gesturing at the chair across from him. "Sit."

I did so, uncomfortably. I could still smell sewage on me, even though I'd showered before changing. I'd have to have another long shower tonight, and help my parents pay the water bill. "Something wrong, Captain Liberty?" I bit my lip.

Captain Liberty stared at me for a second, then shook his head. "No, not at all, Javier. I just wanted to see how you were doing."

"Oh." I blinked. "Um, the doctors had a look at me. They said I'm fine. I'm a little banged up, and I smell kinda gross, but I'm all right."

He smiled a little. "I meant more in general. How are you handling this new life of yours?"

"Oh." I hadn't really thought about it. It was just my life now, and had been for almost a year. "Fine. I mean, I like being part of the Legion."

It was better than what I'd been doing before, which was fighting crime by myself in a makeshift costume designed by Kendall. Until I'd learned that what I was doing was actually against Legion rules, and I could have been classified as a "rogue" and punished for it. Luckily they'd just asked me to join the Legion instead, and given me a fancy costume and training and all the good stuff that came with being a part of a team. I'd never really thought of myself as a team player though.

"That's good," said Captain Liberty. "How is your personal life? You haven't told your parents anything, I assume?"

"No." I shrugged. "Safer that way."

"Indeed. And how is school? Still planning to attend Liberty City University next fall?"

Ugh, why did he *care*? "Yeah, I mean, as long as the Legion's gonna pay for it, I might as well."

"Have you decided what you'll be taking?"

This must have been what holidays were like for people with extended families. Next he was going to start asking me if I had a boyfriend yet. "I thought I'd just do general studies until I figure out what I want to do."

"Well, I hope to see you in my intro to physics class, then."

"Um, yeah." I swallowed. "Of course."

"And how is your training going? Have you been spending time at the gymnasium and our training center?"

"Um. Yeah. Lots."

"Really." He tapped a screen on his desk. "Our records say that you haven't checked in in three months."

If he knew that, why bother to trap me in a lie? I resisted the urge to scowl at him. I was pretty much done being interrogated under the guise of mentor-like concern or whatever. "So what did Wolfhound want? Is there something going on?"

Captain Liberty's dark eyebrows rose a few millimeters. "He is currently concerned that I'm not being honest enough with the Legion members. He feels that I do not perform the role of Captain Liberty to the standards that he would like."

"A lot of people think that, don't they?" I said.

"Well. That's politics for you." Captain Liberty stood and went to open the door, nodding at the view of the city through the tall window behind his desk. "You'd better head home. It will be getting dark soon, and I'm sure your family will be wondering where you are."

Once my costume was clean, I put it on and wore it home, practicing jumping between rooftops and pretending that my stomach wasn't doing stupid somersaults every time I looked down. I stopped on the roof above the café to retrieve my backpack as the sun was setting, glad that no one had found it and decided to rifle through it. Not that I had anything of value in it, unless they were really into science notes and old granola bars.

From there it was only a few blocks to my apartment building, an old dinosaur from the forties. I think it had been nice when it was built, but no one who lived there could afford to keep it up, so the whole thing was kind of falling apart. But we had a little balcony, and my bedroom window opened into an alleyway with a fire escape, so I could come and go out of it without having to worry too much about someone seeing me.

Of course, the minute I got into my bedroom, I heard voices from the living room, which meant that both my parents were already home and probably knew that I wasn't. So then I had to change quickly and put on my glasses (not necessary anymore thanks to superpowers, but still good for hiding my glowing alien eyes and also looking smart), and then go back out the window and down into the alleyway, and then all the way back up the stairs. By the time I got to the apartment, I was about ready to go to sleep for a week.

My mom was in the living room with her feet up, and my dad was frying up something for dinner. I *was* happy to see them, but I was also exhausted, sore, and kind of bummed out, and not really in the mood to talk, even though I always talked to my parents in Spanish, which felt like less work.

"How was your date?" asked my mom, and for a minute I didn't know what she was talking about. I'd completely forgotten about Rick and the nice time we'd had.

"Oh." I stared down at the yellow linoleum and kicked at a broken patch while I hung up my coat. "Yeah, it was good."

"Good?" She sounded concerned. "What's wrong, Javi? You look down."

"No, no, I'm fine, just a long day at school."

"You see, they work these kids too hard," said my dad. "They need to have a nap time, in the afternoon."

"That would be really nice." I swayed a little as I kicked my shoes off.

My mother *tsk*ed. "You must be tired. You want some coffee?"

"I just had coffee." I yawned, still staring at the floor, and shuffled toward the hallway.

"Did he buy it for you?" asked my mom. "Hey, who buys the coffee when it's two boys?"

"We each bought our own coffee, Mama."

"Anyway," said my dad, "it shouldn't always be the boy who buys coffee for the girl. You should think about that, Helena."

I escaped into my bedroom and shut the door, slumping against it. My room was a mess, due to my somewhat compulsive hoarding tendencies. I'd knocked a stack of binders down off my desk coming in through the window, but I didn't have the energy to pick them up. I read somewhere that people with clean living spaces have more energy. But maybe it's people with more energy have cleaner living spaces. Correlation doesn't equal causation, after all.

Anyway, my phone was beeping. I went and collapsed on the bed, picked it up, and got a big jolt of energy when I realized that it was a text from Rick.

Hey Javi! Sorry I had to leave early. I really enjoyed our date. :)

I sat up cross-legged on the bed and typed a reply, trying my best to match his impeccable texting grammar. *I had fun too! It's okay that u had to leave. I did too.*

Well we're both busy guys I guess. :) We should do it again sometime.

I was getting all stupid and excited, and my heart was doing something weird. I actually had my hand on my chest before I realized it and tugged it away. Ew, feelings. I texted Kendall. *I need to temper my expectations.*

I lay back on the bed and grabbed my laptop, glancing out the window while the computer whirred and beeped and took ages to start up.

Wat? Kendall's grammar was much more familiarly butchered. *Hey ur in the news. U didn't miss ur date did u? Bcuz I will bury u.*

I had no idea why Kendall was so invested in my love life, considering the hordes of girls she went through on a regular basis. *No the date was gr8. He's prolly not that into me tho. WHICH is good bcuz ur the 1 that said I should implement a no white boyz rule.*

This white boy is totally the exception, J. He's super sweet, and totes into u. Trust me, I know. ;)

I rolled my eyes and flopped backward onto the bed, holding the phone above my face. *HOW do u know?*

Hush Javi. Ppl talk, I listen. I can't expose my sources.

Whatever

So what did he say? Kendall's text response time was ridiculously fast. Maybe that was her superpower.

He said that he "Really enjoyed our date" and "We should do it again sometime."

Aaaand what did u say?

I haven't responded yet. I flipped back to the conversation with Rick and stared at it. What was I even supposed to say?

My phone buzzed as Kendall replied. *You are killing me rn.*

Okay I'm texting him back.

Good. I want screenshots.

U can wait until tomorrow and steal my phone like u always do.

Make it worth my while then.

I rolled my eyes and texted Rick back as instructed. *Yeah, sounds good. Let me know when is good for you.*

He didn't respond, so I went online and looked for the news article Kendall was talking about. Because I'm a narcissist and I like to read about myself. Shut up.

Blue Spark, a relatively new and mysterious member of the Legion of Liberty, was at the forefront of what first appeared to be a jewelry-store heist downtown today, but soon morphed into a superpowered battle between Legion and Organization representatives . . .

Yadda yadda yadda . . .

Blue Spark has made several appearances in the last six months, and is recognizable by his glowing blue eyes and the markings on his body, which analysts have compared to a Lichtenberg figure, a type of scarring that appears on the body of those who have been struck by lightning. The official Legion database has very little information on Blue Spark, but mentions that his superpowers were acquired from a Kanaan alien. Rumors speculate that there is a connection between the strange markings (possibly scars) that Blue Spark shows off so readily and the unfortunate demise of Kanaan representative and beloved Legion superhero Tuvia, may they rest in peace . . .

The paper wasn't exactly wrong. I had gotten my powers from a Kanaan alien. Tuvia had been in a high-flying battle with an Organization villain when both of them had gone crashing into an electrical station. Meanwhile, some idiot had been climbing on one of the power lines near the station (spoiler: I'm the idiot) and gotten shocked with electricity, which somehow fused my DNA with Tuvia's. Which is cool, except like . . . Tuvia died. And since I skipped out of there before the Legion could find me and figure out what had happened, I never got to meet them. I guess I'm selfish, but it would have been nice to have someone to, you know, explain my powers to me. The rest of the Kanaan barely wanted anything to do with humans, but apparently Tuvia was a pretty cool guy . . . person. Kanaan don't have genders.

Anyway. The news could get really sensationalist fast, which was why all this stuff about my origin wasn't exactly in the public domain. The Legion relied on publicity a lot in order to sell merchandise and get public funding, but the journalists could be pretty damn pushy sometimes, especially considering the code in place about not revealing Legion or Organization members' identities. Junior Heroes especially weren't supposed to give away any information about themselves to news outlets, and the journalists were supposed to keep away from us.

Except sometimes I thought it would be easier to just be like Captain Liberty and not have to worry about having a secret identity. But then I thought about how Captain Liberty's parents died, and how he didn't have any contact with the rest of his family. And then I thought about how being a superhero is kind of a crap deal in the first place, even with the Legion there making it better.

But I guess it wasn't really about me anyway, was it? That was the whole point of being a superhero.

CHAPTER TWO

I t wasn't until I was sitting in second-period science class the next day that I realized with a jolt of horror that the gross toilet-y smell that had been following me around all day wasn't a problem with the school plumbing at all.

It was me.

I don't know if you've ever been in a public place and realized you smelled bad. I really hope not, for your sake, because it's the worst thing in the world, but just imagine it. And then imagine that you're only one step up from a social pariah already, and just trying to make it through senior year without being shoved in a toilet.

And *Oh god, I smelled like a toilet . . . ewwwwww . . .*

So I basically sat there for the second half of class not learning anything, just being secretly paranoid that everyone around me could smell me and was hating me. The moment class was over, I raced to my locker to meet Kendall and wafted my arms in her face.

She raised an eyebrow. "Um, what are you doing?"

"I still smell gross!" I whispered, sniffing my arm. "I can smell it! Smell! Ew!"

"Didn't you shower?"

"Yeah! Like three times!" I really had showered three times. Once at the headquarters, and then again when I got home, and then again in the morning. I'd scrubbed *everywhere*.

"What soap did you use?"

"I don't know. Regular soap?"

Kendall sighed and opened her locker, reaching up to dig through a bunch of bottles and crap on the top shelf. "Here." She pulled out a clear, flower-patterned bottle with what looked like hot-pink petroleum jelly inside. "Use this. It's scented, so it'll at least mask the smell."

I popped it open and gave a sniff, wrinkling my nose as it was assaulted by the olfactory equivalent of the nineties' sleeper hit *Spice World*. "What is this?"

"What? Don't tell me it's threatening to your masculinity."

"What masculinity? I'm just worried at it eating away at my skin." I sniffed it again tentatively.

"It'll take care of the smell," said Kendall. "Now some of us have plans for lunch."

"I'm gonna have a shower right now."

Kendall pinched her mouth to the side. "You sure that's a good idea?"

"No. I guess I could just skip out and go home early."

"Yeah, too bad the school's not being attacked by a mutant crocodile or something, then you could have an excuse to skip class."

"That sounds like a bit more trouble than it's worth."

"For you maybe." Kendall slammed her locker shut. "But at least you'd have a chance to rescue your boy Rick from the jaws of certain death."

"He's not my boy!" I shouted after her as she left, and then immediately felt self-conscious for yelling. I stared down at the pink bottle in my hand and brought my arm to my nose again. Yeah, a shower was definitely in order.

Unfortunately the only showers available at school were the public ones adjacent to the men's locker room. I hadn't set foot in the gymnasium wing of the school since I'd finished my last year of mandatory PE, and was paranoid that I'd be spotted and called out as the unathletic nerd I was (and that I wouldn't be able to shower without a bunch of dudes staring at my, um, assets), but luckily the whole wing was nearly deserted.

Now, don't get me wrong, I'm not self-conscious about my body at all. The accident that gave me my powers and markings also gave me a pretty awesome set of abs. It's upsetting to me that I'm never able to show them off, because, you know, glowing lightning scars. I make up for it by wearing a revealing costume, but it's not really the same. I sometimes fantasize that a hot guy would happen upon me in the showers and notice how sexy I am, and, you know, things would progress from there.

Except that I don't even like jocks. Well, except Rick. For some reason.

Anyway, showering in a public bathroom where anyone could walk in and see me was really, really stupid. But I couldn't stand the idea of smelling like crap any longer, and I didn't want to skip either. With my luck, Captain Liberty would probably pull up his "records" and see that I had, then drag me into his office for another "talk."

I would just be quick. In and out, scrub myself down, and then back into my clothes before anyone came in and noticed.

Yeah, *right*.

So there I was, in the big empty shower, trying to wipe myself down and get as clean as possible, or at least get enough of the pink stuff on myself to mask the smell. (Why would I rather smell like Princess Sparkle than sewer, you ask? Because I, my friend, am unashamed of my sexuality. Also because I'm not an idiot.) And then I heard a bunch of shouting and rowdy noises and doors opening and then, yep, you guessed it, a bunch of football players came barging into the locker room, heading straight for the showers.

I'd left my bag with my clothes, towel, glasses, and special color-changing contacts from the Legion (since I'm not supposed to get them wet) in the locker room, of course. I couldn't go running out there stark naked with glowing blue everything to get it, but the alternative was waiting there for them to all come in and see me. And at that moment, I didn't even care about them finding out about my secret identity. I was honestly worried about them seeing my markings and my weird glowing eyes and thinking that I looked like a *freak*.

I did the only thing I could think of, which was to jump up to the ceiling and pull off one of the weird Styrofoam tiles and climb in behind it. I'd just managed to put it back as the football players came flooding into the showers, and I was left sitting there, supporting my weight on the fragile metal beams, peering down through a crack in the tiles at a bunch of naked men.

Oh.

The little space above the ceiling tiles began to glow bright blue as my entire body heated up. I could practically hear myself buzzing with embarrassment and, well, other things.

I should probably mention now that I had actually had sex before that point. Once. Or rather, Blue Spark had. It was some guy I'd saved from a collapsing theater. He wanted to repay me for saving his life. I was pretty sure he hadn't realized I was a teenager. I kept the mask on the whole time. It was . . . enlightening. And awkward. There, you're all caught up.

Anyway, football players. Yeah, okay, I was enjoying this a bit more than I should have. I was terrified that one of them would look up and see me somehow, or that I would fall through the ceiling or something. But there was nothing I could do except wait, and watch, so . . . what else was I supposed to do?

They all got under the showerheads, laughing and joking around with each other in their dumb jock voices. That *should* have been a turnoff, it really should have been, but it was hard to be distracted when the bodies were right there and . . .

"Hey, have you guys seen Javier? I think this is his bag."

That sounded like Rick. I jumped, and nearly fell through the ceiling, craning my head to try to see through the crack. It was definitely Rick, although I couldn't see him to tell if he was naked or not. Not that it mattered. Ahem.

"Who, Jav-ver?" laughed one of the other jocks. "What's with that kid, anyway? Why do you like him?"

"Because I do," said Rick. "Seriously, this is his bag, and his clothes are in it. He must be here."

My mind was going into full panic mode now. I'd put my clothes in the top of the bag, but if Rick dug any deeper, he'd uncover my costume, and then I'd be screwed.

"Dude, I think we'd notice if he was in here," said another guy. Or maybe the same one. It was hard to tell them apart. "Maybe he's hiding like a little bi—"

"Hey, that's the guy I'm dating," said Rick, making my heart swell a little. "What, are you jealous?" That prompted a bunch of jeering and laughing. I caught sight of Rick, sadly fully clothed still, making his way through the showers and looking around. Finally, sounding a little concerned, he said, "Well, I guess I'll take these to the lost and found, then."

Of course then I started to seriously freak out. This was absolutely the stupidest thing I'd done in the history of ever, and that included climbing up an electrical tower after a pair of thirty-dollar shoes. Rick would take my bag to the lost and found, and I would be trapped here, probably forever. Or at least until night when I could sneak, naked, into the lost and found, and hope that no one checked the security cameras. Great, this was just great.

Rick left the showers, and I heard his footsteps stop as he reached the locker room doors. "Hey, Kendall, have you seen Javi?"

Kendall? Was she here to rescue me?

"Yeah." Kendall's tone was pretty darn standoffish considering how she'd been gushing about him before. "He's taking a shower."

"Yeah? He's not in there, though, but his clothes are in this bag."

I heard Kendall grab the bag from Rick, and he protested. There was a moment of silence while she riffled through it, and presumably found my suit, and then the noise of her zipping it back up. "We should leave it in there. You probably just weren't looking hard enough for him."

Her footsteps came into the locker room, causing a loud protest from every single guy in there.

"Relax!" she shouted. "I'm gay, I don't care about your dicks."

"Kendall, you seriously can't be in here." Rick sounded as if Kendall had just made him an accomplice in an accidental bank heist. "This is the men's locker room!"

"Is it?" Kendall sounded nonplussed. "Javier, are you in here?"

"Get the hell out!" hollered a guy. "And take your little boyfriend with you."

"Hey, you can shut your hole!" Kendall yelled back, and then more quietly: "He's gotta be here somewhere. We should just leave his bag."

"I've looked in every one of the stalls though," said Rick. "There's nowhere he could be. What if something's happened to him?"

"I'm sure he's fine." I could tell that she was worried and trying not to show it. "There's no point in moving his bag, anyway. Maybe he'll come back to it."

"Yeah." Rick sounded unconvinced. "Maybe." He let out a weak laugh. "I mean, it's not as if he's running around campus naked."

"Right," said Kendall, and her footsteps receded. I couldn't see much, but I was sure every guy in there was breathing a sigh of relief and uncovering his junk. Which, I mean, stupidest thing ever. Kendall didn't even like guys and Rick did, but they didn't seem to care about him.

Anyway, so at least my bag was being left in the locker room, but I was still trapped up in the ceiling with, like, every part of my body cramping. And the excitement of seeing a bunch of naked guys was starting to wear off. High school guys are just not as impressive as certain adult movies might suggest. And when Rick finally got in the shower, he went and did it in the corner where I couldn't even see, so there was really absolutely no benefit to the situation whatsoever.

And then everyone just sort of wandered off in unison, like this big jock herd. They asked Rick if he wanted to come with them to lunch, and he said no. So then it was just him in the locker room, and me with the little sharp metal bars of the ceiling digging into my knees, waiting for him to leave.

But instead he was all, "Javier? Are you in here? They're gone now."

I didn't respond, hoping he'd give up and leave. I didn't know back then how freaking stubborn he can be.

"Seriously," he continued. "Javi, I know you must be in here. You wouldn't go running off without your phone and your wallet and stuff. Are you sick?" He wandered around the now-empty locker room, his footsteps echoing. "Javvieeerrrr . . ."

I sighed, and did my best to throw my voice so that he couldn't tell where it was coming from. "Yeah, okay, I'm here, but I don't want you to see me."

Rick stopped walking and turned around, so the voice thing must have worked pretty well. I'd have to test that out on bad guys sometime. "What? Javi, where are you? Are you okay?"

"I'm fine." I was not fine. "Could you just . . . go away for a bit? Until I can get dressed."

Rick was silent. He was probably either thinking *He's naked, eyyy!* or else *Oh my god he threw up all over himself. Gross.* I like to think it was the first one, but I'm sure we all know better. "Yeah," he said finally. "Okay, I'll meet you outside."

"Promise you won't watch?"

"Yeah, I promise. I'm not a creep."

I didn't think he was a creep. I mean, he hadn't been kicked off the football team for peeping or anything. (If anything I was the Peeping Tom, but that was part of the reason I wasn't on the football team. Yeah, *that* was the reason.) So probably it was fine. Not that I even minded him seeing me naked, or wouldn't have if it weren't for, well, you know. But I listened to him walk to the door and shout "Okay, I'm gone!" and shut it before I jumped down from the ceiling and rushed into my clothes as quickly as I ever had in my life.

I didn't bother to put my suit on underneath my clothes. I definitely didn't feel like fighting crime right now. But I put my contacts back in and set them to brown (if you're wondering, before I got in touch with the Legion, I went around wearing cheap colored contacts and sunglasses a lot). I stared at myself in the mirror for a bit, trying to school my face into a casual *Oh, I was just hanging out in the shower ceiling, no reason* face, and come up with some sort of excuse. Unfortunately, *I puked all over myself* was actually sounding pretty good. I was mostly just hoping that Rick wouldn't ask.

He didn't. Instead, when I came out into the hallway, he put his hand on my shoulder, all comforting, and leaned in. His hand felt big and strong, and even though I could probably take him in a fight, it made me feel kinda warm and safe. I actually got this, like, rush of emotion at that point, because I hadn't had a great couple of days, and now here was Rick, all sincere and concerned about me, and it was just really nice.

"Hey," he said softly.

"Hi." I swallowed. My voice was all stupid and wobbly. "Um . . ."

"Sorry." He took his hand away. "I was worried about you. Are you okay, are you sick?"

"I'm fine."

"You don't need to go home early?"

"Ah." I pulled away reluctantly. "No, I'll just rest after school."

"How are you getting home?"

"I'll walk." I shrugged. "It's only a few blocks."

"No way." Rick frowned. "I'll drive you."

I felt kind of guilty for playing sick or whatever, even though I'd said I was fine, but I wasn't going to turn down a ride from Rick. "Okay."

Rick's phone rang. He pulled it out of his pocket and glanced at it, brow furrowed. "Sorry, I have to take this. But I'll meet you in the parking lot after school, okay? Don't walk home." He answered the phone and jogged off. I stared after him in a daze.

Then Kendall appeared out of nowhere, nearly bowling me over. "Oh my god, where were you? I was freaking out."

"I'm fine." I watched Rick run away, hunched over and muttering into his phone. "I was showering and then the whole freaking football team came in, so I had to hide in the ceiling."

"I thought you'd been kidnapped or something," said Kendall angrily. "I called the Legion."

"What? Seriously?"

"Yeah, sorry, I was really worried."

"Great." I turned as Rick rounded a corner and shoved my hands in my pockets, heading for the cafeteria. Kendall followed me.

"Hey, don't get mad at me! It's my job to worry about you. Anyway, you'll wanna hear what they told me."

"I'm not mad at you." I huffed. This day was getting better and better. "What did they say?"

"That if you were missing after a couple of days, they had methods in place to locate you."

"That's so vague."

"Exactly. So I pressed them about it. Turns out, you have a chip implanted in your butt."

"Hey, I know. Don't talk about my butt!"

"Uh, you didn't mind me talking about your butt when you wanted me to design you a supersuit that showed it off."

"It did really show it off." I sighed wistfully.

"It did," agreed Kendall. "The crap they have you in now isn't half as stylish as my original design. At least they kept the color scheme."

"Uh-huh. So, what about the chip in my butt? I remember getting it. It's not something you forget."

"What, having something stuck in your butt?"

We made it to the cafeteria and slipped in, heading to stand in the lunch line behind a group of hipsters.

"I feel like that was some sort of joke," I said. "But I'm not getting it. Maybe you could elaborate."

"Yeah, maybe you could tell me why you were fine with"—she lowered her voice so as not to be overheard by the girls in front of us—"the Legion sticking a tracking chip in you."

"I don't know." I shrugged, uncomfortable. "It was just something they did. They gave me like a million other shots too, and I had to sign a bunch of stuff. It's not like I really had a choice."

"Uh-huh. They're freaking sketchy, you know that?"

"Yeah, I know." We stepped up to grab our trays and be presented with whatever delicacies the cafeteria had to offer us today. "But they're a better alternative than the Organization. I'm not going to not use my powers to help people just because I don't want a chip in my butt."

The only real good thing about the rest of the school day was that I no longer smelled like sewage. Kendall's soap had done the trick, and I smelled like a preteen girl instead. Definitely superior, although still not ideal. But if Rick noticed that I was making the inside of his SUV smell like candy on the drive home, he didn't mention it.

"It's cool that you can drive," I said as we pulled out of the school parking lot.

"Yeah." Rick sounded pleased. "I learned when I was like thirteen. My family all used to drive out to the lake house, do spins in the gravel pit."

"Sounds dangerous."

"Definitely. I'm way more responsible with driving now. And I have my license."

"Your family has a lake house?"

Rick must have noticed the hint of jealousy in my voice, because he seemed embarrassed. "My extended family. We share it. It's not fancy or anything. This one guy has a whole mansion out there, with a swimming pool and everything. What's the point of that, right?"

"Maybe he's afraid of the mutant fish."

Rick snorted. "That's a myth."

"Nuh-uh." I turned in my seat. "I did a science presentation on the weird stuff that happened at the power plant out there. The water's radioactive."

"It is not!" Rick protested. "Look, I swam in it every summer since I was a kid, do you see any mutant gills?"

"Like you'd show them off."

"Actually, that sounds awesome, I totally would."

"What if they were, like, somewhere inappropriate?"

Rick sucked on his teeth. "I don't know. I'd probably still let people see them. For science."

"Right." I grinned. "For science."

"So where exactly do you live?"

"Oh." I felt my face fall. Rick was driving this obviously expensive (if sort of old) SUV, and talking about his family's lake house, for crying out loud, and now he was gonna have to drive down crap street and drop me off in front of my apartment, which might as well just take the opportunity to collapse on top of us. "Twenty-second Street? You don't have to take me all the way there—"

"It's on my way to work. I'll drop you off." He paused. "I just want to make sure you get home okay."

"Yeah. Thanks."

We stopped at a red light, and Rick glanced over at me. "Javier. You know if people at school are giving you a hard time—"

"They're not."

"Well . . ." Rick seemed a bit lost for words. "If they try to. Don't let it bother you."

I looked at him, eyebrows raised. "Easy for *you* to say. You're normal."

He raised his eyebrows right back. "Are you not normal?"

A bit of excitement and fear tickled through me. I could tell him right now. Just tell him everything. Except for the fact that was a really, really stupid idea, of course.

"Well yeah," I said instead, "sure, but they don't think so."

He put the SUV back in gear and turned down Twenty-second Street. Imagining it how Rick must be seeing it, I noticed things like graffiti, how the buildings were close together, and the places where metal fences were broken and the bricks in the old buildings were chipped. Not that I hadn't noticed these things before, and I honestly didn't know why I cared, except that I kind of wanted to impress Rick, or at least not make him feel bad for me. I hated thinking that maybe he was just going out with me because he felt bad for me. But I couldn't imagine why else he would be.

"Nothing wrong with not being normal," said Rick.

I scoffed. "Maybe if you're all cool and popular to start with. If you're not, then, you know. People just think you're weird. This is me." I gestured at my apartment. "You can pull over here."

"I don't think you're weird, Javier."

"We-ell." I grabbed my bag from the floor and opened the door. "You probably don't know me very well, then. Thanks for the ride." I did my best to grin at him, and he gave me a halfhearted smile back. I dropped the grin as soon as he pulled away, and I watched him drive off.

I climbed the stairs slowly, *thunking* from side to side with each step and contemplating all the ways in which I was a loser who was definitely going to die alone. I had no idea why I was being so standoffish and rude to Rick. If I were him, I'd be running the other way. He was probably driving to work right now and thinking about all the other nice, normal, nonprickly guys he could date instead of me. And I couldn't even blame him.

My dad was home, sitting on the couch with the TV on, a newspaper open on the couch beside him, and the motherboard of a computer spread out in pieces on the coffee table. "Hey, Javi!" he said as I hung up my coat. "Plans for tonight?"

I shrugged. "Just homework."

"Did you see that boy again? I'm asking because your mother wants to know."

For a moment I wanted to confess how crappy it made me feel that his family had so much more money than mine. Then I came to my senses and realized how awful that would make my dad feel. "Yeah, he's nice."

My dad nodded, and went back to his motherboard. I kicked my shoes off and went to my bedroom, shut the door behind me, and flopped down on the bed.

The thing is, my parents work crazy hard for everything we have, and they're pretty fiercely proud of it. For me to feel embarrassed by it almost felt like betraying them. A bit of pride and defiance flared up in me, and for a moment, I was annoyed that Rick had made me feel embarrassed. But then, he hadn't done it on purpose. It certainly wasn't his fault that he was rich.

I huffed and blew a strand of hair out of my face, and then got up to take off the layers of clothes I was wearing, suddenly feeling a bit claustrophobic. I checked that my door was locked before pulling off my T-shirt and examining the now-familiar glowing lines on my body. They branched out from my core, concentrating mostly on my stomach and hips, but trailing up over my shoulders and down my arms as well. I slid my fingers along the lines, and they pulsed as I did so. Below my hips was where I was most embarrassed about. The markings concentrated there, turning me into something I almost didn't recognize. Something distinctly nonhuman.

My phone buzzed in my bag, and I jumped, feeling vaguely guilty, and rushed to check it. It was a message from the Legion, asking if I was available for patrol tonight.

No, I texted, sitting down on the bed. *I have homework.*

You are required to log at least fifteen hours of patrol a week. You have currently logged seven and a half.

I know.

It is Thursday.

I KNOW. I glared at the screen. *Fine, but I'll bring my homework with me.*

Excellent. The posting is for Market and Fifteenth Street. Please review the intersection, and be ready to respond to calls.

I sighed and got up to get dressed. *Are you even human?* I texted petulantly. *Or am I taking orders from a machine?*

I'm human. My name is Beth.

Oh. Sorry for snapping at you Beth. I've been having a bad day.

Understandable. Enjoy patrol.

I told my dad I'd been called into my fake Pizza Hut job, and took the bus down to Fifteenth and Market. Then I changed behind a dumpster and climbed a fire escape. Liberty City has a lot of fire escapes. Apparently they installed a bunch of them in the forties to help superheroes get around. Well, and to help people escape fires, presumably.

Then I sat up on the roof, reading my chemistry chapters and sort of glancing down at the intersection occasionally. At one point I saw what I thought was a guy trying to mug some chick, but when I went to look closer, they were making out, which I definitely did not need to see. I went back and sat on the edge of the building, reading about electrons and photons. Mostly stuff that, if I was being honest, I already knew. Not that I was, like, a super genius or anything. I just knew some science. It probably didn't hurt that my dad was a computer whiz either. Anyway, it doesn't matter when you're in school. I still had to read the chapters, and they were so . . . freaking . . . boring.

I ended up lying on my back with my knees hooked over the side of the building, reading my book upside down and paying absolutely no attention to the intersection. That was when I saw the guy.

He was standing in the window of a tall office building a few blocks away. And not, like, on the floor inside the building, just chilling and glancing out the window. Like, actually on the windowsill, staring down, and not looking very happy about it at all.

Crap.

I stood and tossed my book to the side, shoved my phone into one of the pouches on my belt, and raced across the roof, jumping a couple of gaps to get to the building across from the man in the window. He must have noticed me land because his head jerked up. He was a bit too far away to see his expression, but I thought he looked scared.

"Uh," I shouted. "Hi. Whatcha doing?"

I desperately hoped that he was just, like, cleaning . . . or something. Because I had no idea how to deal with someone who was trying to jump. I wondered if the Legion offered classes on the subject, but it was kind of too late for that now.

"Nothing!" the guy squeaked. "It's fine."

"You sure?" I leaned over the side of the building. "Maybe you wanna go back inside, it's not really safe out there."

The guy laughed nervously, and glanced back inside the building. And then a low threatening voice said, "Tell him you're just getting fresh air."

"It's fine," said the man again. "Just getting . . . f-fresh air—"

But I'd already jumped across. I was intending to grab the guy and wrap myself around him so that we'd both roll safely in through the window, but then a gloved hand reached out and snagged him around the ankle. In the second before I hit him, the hand pulled him back inside and slammed the window shut in front of me.

I had just enough time to bring my hands up and send shock waves to break the glass before I crashed through the window and rolled into the room. It took a minute for me to get my bearings, and I noticed the thick green carpet underneath me before anything else. Then someone grabbed me by the shoulder and hoisted me painfully up, and I was looking into the masked face of Jimmy Black.

"You!" I resisted the urge to spit on him. "What the hell are you doing here?"

"Wouldn't you like to know?" Jimmy sneered at me, and then snapped his fingers at the henchman holding me. The guy let go of my shoulder and aimed a punch to my gut, but I managed to twist out of the way and send him skidding across the room with another shock wave.

Jimmy looked annoyed. He jerked his head at the second henchman guy, who reached into a cupboard and pulled out a big black safe. He hoisted it onto his shoulders and rushed from the room, and I moved to go after him, but then Jimmy went to the man by the window, and I didn't want to leave him alone with a civilian. He was a middle-aged guy, balding, business suit, completely innocuous. He was pleading "No, no please, don't!" as Jimmy grabbed him and lifted him up by the leg, all casually.

"I will ask you one more time." He sounded deadly serious. "What is the pass code to the safe?"

The guy didn't say anything. Instead he just turned to me, all panicky, and whispered, "Help."

Jimmy broke the guy's leg, twisting it so that it bent backward with a loud crack.

The guy screamed as Jimmy dropped him. He hit the ground hard, and Jimmy glowered at me as he followed his henchmen out the door. I wanted to go after him, but Legion rules say to always tend to civilians first, so I went to the guy and knelt beside him, trying to remember the basic first aid stuff I'd been taught.

He shook his head at me, his face red and teary. "No! Go after them, get back what they took!"

"What did they take?"

The guy shook his head again and grabbed his leg. "No time to explain. Go!"

I didn't need much convincing. I gave the guy what I hoped was a concerned look, and then I was up and off, running down the hallway after Jimmy Black and his henchmen. They were at the elevator, cool as you please, just stepping in as I tore out the door and into the hallway. Jimmy grinned at me as the doors closed and I ran full tilt into them, my ears ringing from the impact. I gripped the doors with my gloves and managed to pry them open, straining every muscle in my body.

The elevator had already gone, of course, but I'd seen this particular trick plenty of times in movies. By the way, one of the things they briefed us on at the Legion was not to rely too heavily on anything you see in a movie. Which was crap: I learned everything I needed to know about being a superhero from movies. Including the part where all elevators have a little door in the ceiling.

I jumped down, and landed heavily on the top of the moving elevator. I hoped they heard me inside, and were *terrified*. I know I was terrified enough for all of us. I hadn't really been able to appreciate before then just how fast elevators go. So anyway, I pulled the little hatch open, but before I could jump in, Jimmy Black burst out onto the top and tried to throw me into the cables. I barely managed to twist around his fist (I'm good at twisting) and grab the top of the elevator to avoid skidding against the wall. I pulled myself forward and used my momentum to slam into him, pressing him up against the wall instead. He screamed and fell forward. I slithered down into the elevator just as it landed and the henchmen rushed out.

I followed them through the crowded lobby, and almost caught them before Jimmy Black's hand landed on my shoulder, pulling me around for a punch to the face.

Ouch, by the way. The crowd around us gasped (there's always a crowd) so it must have looked pretty impressive. I wiped my mouth, tasting blood, and spat some at him. "Ugh! First you made me swim around in crap, and now this? What's your deal?"

Jimmy shrugged nonchalantly. "You're the one who interrupted my business. Shit happens. You should get a waterproof suit, like me." He lunged at me, but I managed to dodge him this time, barely. He was fast.

"I wasn't exactly expecting to go into the sewers," I said. "Anyway, they don't give Junior Heroes waterproof suits."

"Junior?" Jimmy laughed. "How old are you?"

"Seventeen."

"Seventeen!" Jimmy laughed again. He dodged a shock wave that I sent at him, taking advantage of my momentary concentration to dash forward and grab me around the neck. "Legion sends kids to do their work now, eh?"

"I'm not a kid," I managed to choke out, but his hands were crushing my airway. As he leaned over me, I realized I had an advantage, albeit an underhanded one.

I used a shock wave to launch my knee toward his crotch. Jimmy screamed, more from anger than pain I think, but his hands loosened on my neck for a moment, enough for me to slip away, anyway.

What happened next was entirely not my fault. Having been a victim of a kick to the crotch on more than one occasion, I thought I had a pretty good idea of the amount of time needed to recover from one. I couldn't have possibly known that Jimmy Black apparently has balls of steel. So when I was looking around for where his henchman with the safe had gone, assuming that Jimmy was still bent over and cursing my ancestors, he was instead grabbing a desk (yes, you read that right, a freaking *desk*) and swinging it at me.

The impact sent me across the room and into the wall, which crumbled under me. The desk came flying after me, doing further damage to the wall, and I barely managed to roll out of the way before it crashed to the floor.

Every single bone in my body hurt. I mean it. Every single one. I just lay there for a moment, wheezing, while a few brave souls rushed over to see if I was okay. I was, obviously. When am I not okay? Well, a lot, but this time I was (relatively) okay. But by the time I got up and rushed through the door, Jimmy Black was completely out of sight, and no one could tell me where he or his henchmen had gone.

So, I'm gonna skip ahead to the next day, because you really don't need to read all about me being dragged into the Legion headquarters and treated for, like, a full-body concussion or something, and lectured endlessly about how I should have called for backup. Then I had to go home and make up a story to my parents about how I'd tripped and fallen into an oven door at work. Like, one of those big metal pizza ovens? They have big doors. I thought it was a good excuse.

And then my dad was like, "Oh, you need to file a worker's report about this. You could have been really badly hurt!" I *was* really badly hurt, and I must have looked like it, but I had to just play it off and pretend it wasn't that bad, when what I really needed was my mom to make me hot chocolate and, like, sing to me or something. Shut up, you would too.

Anyway, so the next day I was back at school, bruises all covered up in layers and layers of clothes, like usual, and Kendall was chatting at me while I was trying to pay attention in math class. I'd texted her basically everything that had happened the night before, but she wasn't satisfied to leave it at that. "What do you think was in the safe?"

"I don't know," I waved her off as I wrote down formulas. "Well, I have an idea, but you're not going to like it."

"Javier." Mr. Bruce turned around and glared at me. "Do you have something to say?"

"Sir, Kendall was distracting me."

Kendall glared at me. "Way to throw me under the bus, homie. Sir, Javier's face was distracting me."

"Do you two need to be separated?"

"I need to be separated from humanity." I ducked down to continue copying from the board.

"Well, let's hope that won't be necessary." Mr. Bruce went back to the blackboard.

Kendall poked me with her pencil and slid a blank piece of paper over to me.

No! I scribbled. *Damning evidence!*

She rolled her eyes. *Write it in Spanish.*

Spanish is not an unbreakable code.

Sure it is. Exactly zero other students here speak it.

Yeah, including you.

Kendall gestured at her phone under the desk. *I have Google translate.*

$BC2 + AC2 = AB \times BH$ *and* $AC2 = AB \times AH$

U SUCK JAVIER. :p

NOT RECENTLY. :PPPP

After class I told her what I was worried about. As if I'd had a choice. It was like that when I was trying to keep my powers a secret from her too. Resistance is futile.

"I think it's the tracking chips."

Kendall's face went into an appropriate O.O shape. "Seriously? Why?"

"Because." I leaned against my locker, lowering my voice. Having superhearing gives you the unfortunate feeling that everyone else does too and is listening to what you're saying. "Wolfhound was arguing with Captain Liberty about them, after the jewelry-store thing. Captain Liberty said that what was stolen could be potentially dangerous to everyone in the Legion, and Wolfhound said something like 'Oh, it's the chips, isn't it?'"

"So, what, they're stealing . . . more chips?"

"I think they're stealing something that will help them use them. Like, to locate everyone in the Legion, no matter where they are."

The thought made me queasy. I hadn't really thought much of having a tracking chip in me before, but that was when I'd known for sure that it would only ever be the Legion using it. The idea of someone, especially someone from the Organization, having access to every single Legion member's location was really scary.

"Javier." Kendall sounded deadly serious. "That's *really* bad. You need to tell Captain Liberty."

"I'm sure he already knows."

"And what is he doing about it?"

"I have no idea. Stuff, I assume."

"Stuff." Kendall raised an eyebrow.

"Well, he doesn't tell me, I'm just a Junior Hero— Crap, it's Rick."

Rick strode up to us with a big smile on his face, and I was panicking, like full-on about to hyperventilate.

"Rick!" I shouted. "Whaa— How d-did you know where my locker was?"

Rick just shook his head at me. "We go to the same school, Javi. Why wouldn't I know where your locker was?"

"He's stalking you," said Kendall to me, matter-of-factly.

"What?" Rick's smile was strained. "Whoa, hey, I'm not stalking anyone."

"Relax." Kendall grinned at us. "You two are adorable."

"You're not," I replied. "Go make someone else awkward."

"Right." Kendall grabbed her stuff, still with a big smile on her face. "I'll give you guys your space." She winked at me and slammed her locker shut, off to help/hinder someone else's love life, no doubt.

I don't think Rick had ever been more confused in his life. I could tell he wanted to say something, but probably didn't want to offend me by insulting my friend.

"Yeah." I gave him a break. "She's a little weird."

"She's . . ." Rick paused for a staggeringly long amount of time. "Definitely her own person." He nodded like he'd just made the most groundbreaking assessment of all time.

"Sometimes I feel like we're all part of this, like, high school fantasy fan fiction, and she's writing it," I supplied, and his face split into a grin.

"Ch'yeah, exactly. So, uh." He kicked his foot on the ground. "Plans after school?"

"None." I probably still had a few hours left before I made my quota of fifteen for the week, but after yesterday, I really didn't care. "You?"

"I was gonna take a drive up to the point, actually. Watch the sunset. Do you—" he paused and glanced up at me with a smile "—wanna come?"

So that was how I ended up in Rick's car again, only this time we were winding up the little dirt road on Freedom Hill. I'd only ever been to the top of the hill once before, on a school hiking trip, and it'd been foggy and rainy and generally gross that day, so we hadn't even been able to see the view. It was nice and sunny this time though, and every now and then I'd catch a glimpse of the city between the trees as we drove.

I turned my phone to silent and shoved it in my bag, smiling at Rick. He was wearing a black T-shirt with the school logo on it, and his arms looked great. I wished I could take my sweater off too.

"You wanna listen to some music?" asked Rick, and I nodded. He passed me his iPod. "Here, plug this in. Find something you like."

He mostly had rock songs, although there was also a surprising amount of folk music, and Europop. I settled on a Mumford & Sons album.

"What's on your iPod?" he asked, and I shrugged.

"Well, for starters, I don't have an iPod." I reached into my bag to dig out my old battered MP3 player.

Rick raised an eyebrow. "Wow, that thing is hard-core. Does it take batteries?"

"Yep. I think they're dead though." I checked. "Yep."

"You don't listen to music much?"

"Not really. I guess I like peace and quiet."

"What else do you like?"

"Uh." I squinted at him sideways. "That's a vague question."

"Well, give me something to go on, here. I'm trying to get to know you." Rick nodded his head in time with the banjo. "Okay, tell me something notable about your past."

I leaned forward and rested my hand on my chin. "Well, I moved to America when I was five. I didn't speak any English when I started school. I hated it."

"Did we go to the same elementary school?"

"I don't think so. You'd remember me. I was the weird kid everyone loved to hate on."

"Oh come on, I'm sure everyone didn't hate you."

"They did, for real." I tilted my head at him, chin still resting on my hand. "You're one of those people who don't believe that, like, bullying actually happens, aren't you?"

"I don't know." Rick rolled his neck. "I mean, I believe that kids can be awful to each other. I guess I've just never actually seen it happen."

"No, because they wait until no one's watching."

"People say mean stuff to each other sometimes, but I always saw that as more of a reflection on themselves than on the person they're talking to."

I gazed out the window. The sun was getting close to the horizon. "You don't get it. Seriously."

"Tell me, then."

I glanced at Rick. He was studying me earnestly. Then he had to turn away again to focus on the road.

"I don't know." I leaned back on the seat. "Like, a year ago my parents finally bought me shoes that I actually wanted. They spent a decent amount of money to get me nice new ones. And I guess they looked really fancy compared to all my other clothes, because some kids noticed and followed me home and—" I sighed, and rolled my eyes, feeling uncomfortable "—they knocked me down, pulled my shoes off, tied the laces together, and threw them onto an electrical cord."

"Seriously?" Rick's eyes were wide. "They did that? Did you tell anyone?"

I shook my head. "I went and got them back. It was stupid, but you know, I didn't want my parents to know. And then I—" I paused "—fell. Off the wire."

"Holy. Were you okay?"

"Uh. More or less."

I hadn't fallen of course. I'd been knocked off by an electrical current so strong it should have killed me. I'd dragged myself home, smoking and glowing and crying because there was a bunch of stuff in my brain that hadn't been there before and that didn't make sense (side effect of the DNA transfer, the Legion had told me later). And I'd hid everything from everyone with big sweaters and crappy contacts and sunglasses, in no small part because I hadn't wanted anyone to know about the stupid thing with the shoes.

"The point is, I never told anyone because I knew if they got in trouble, they'd take it out on me. Better just to try to fix things myself and not mention it."

Rick gritted his teeth. "That's . . . that's really awful. I'm sorry that happened to you, Javier."

I shrugged. "It's all right. Just you acknowledging it is something."

"I feel like I've lived a charmed life compared to you. I've had some bad things happen but, I never, uh—"

"What?" I pressed him, sure that he'd been about to say something.

"Ah." He rolled his shoulders again. "About a year ago, I was out driving back from a camping trip with a couple of friends, and, uh, I guess something ran out in front of us." He rubbed his neck. "I mean, to tell the truth, I don't even really remember what it was, or the trip at all. I woke up in the hospital with my memories all fuzzy."

"Seriously? Were your friends okay?"

Rick glanced sideways at me. "No. The car was totaled. My friend Josh . . . he didn't make it. They found his girlfriend, though, wandering around like three days later. They don't know how she made it out. They said they had to pry Josh and me out—" He stopped abruptly. "Uh, yeah, so that happened."

"Only a year ago?" I tried to remember if he'd missed school, if anyone in school had even known about it happening. "Were you . . . hurt?"

"No, just a bump on the head. Vanessa was fine too." He rubbed his nose. "At least, physically. I think she's in Liberty Fields now."

Liberty Fields Care Home was where Liberty City's chronically mentally ill went. There were also a lot of older people there from the time in the eighties when the Organization ran Liberty City. Like, people who had been tortured and kidnapped and controlled by them. I'd never visited anyone there, but the place freaked me out whenever I went by it.

"God." I stared at Rick as he drove. The sun was lower now, and we were almost to the top of the hill. "I'm so sorry. That's, like, *awful.*"

"It was pretty bad," Rick admitted. "But, you know, I survived. As weird as it sounds, I feel like I got a kind of purpose out of it. Everything got clearer: I realized what I needed to do with my life."

"What's that?"

Rick turned to look at me, seriously. Then he smiled a bit. "Play football, obviously."

"Ha!" I laughed, grateful for the defusion of tension. It was a bit stuffy in the car, and Rick rolled the windows down as we drove up to one of the parking spots on the point. Over the low wooden fence, Liberty City was visible, the sun setting behind it, lighting the windows and shining towers on fire. I could see the Legion headquarters, a towering glass building rising up above all the others. The large L emblazoned on the top glowed in the sunlight, and it seemed to be watching over the city. It helped that it was built on a bit of a hill. I could also see the older areas of the city across the river, picturesque from so far away and, beyond them, the forest following the river down the rest of the valley.

"It's beautiful." I unbuckled my seat belt to see better. "I think I can see my apartment."

"My house is over there too," said Rick. "I never could figure out which one it was though."

I leaned on the dashboard, moving forward to see farther. I could feel Rick's eyes on me as I bent forward, and I almost blushed. I sort of liked it, though. I glanced over at him and grinned, causing him to blush instead.

"Uh." He looked uncomfortable. "Sorry."

I sat back. "For what?"

"Nothing." Rick didn't seem to know what to do with his hands. He rubbed them together, patted the steering wheel, touched the back of his neck. "I mean, I'm just glad you agreed to come up here with me."

I fought the urge to hunch forward again. "Do you . . . actually like me?"

"What? Of course! Why would I ask you out if I didn't?"

"It's just"—I gestured at myself—"I know I'm not, like, much of a catch."

"I think you're *gorgeous.*" The way he said it, all serious and passionate, sent a shiver down my spine. He was still blushing a little, his neck and face tinged pink. "Really, I even like your glasses and your big sweaters and everything. And I like how you are."

He seemed to be having trouble expressing himself a bit, but he charged on. "Everyone else is so preoccupied with school, it's like it's the only thing about them. But you seem like . . . like more. Like you're ready for things to get better, instead of trying to hold on to something that isn't that great anyway . . ." He grimaced and turned his head away. "Sorry, I guess that's all kind of presumptuous."

I didn't think it was presumptuous at all. He'd described me better than I'd ever been able to describe myself. Plus, he thought I was gorgeous? It was lucky I didn't explode from ego right there. "It's true though. No one's ever said it like that before, but you're right. Things will get better. I'll make them better."

The sun glowed orange on the horizon, blinding me, and I squinted and reached up to pull my shade down at the same time as Rick did. Our hands touched. My heart started to beat all fast. It was very cliché. And then Rick slid his hand down my arm and touched the side of my face.

I was terrified. I was terrified he'd look into my eyes and see them glowing blue behind the contacts. I was terrified he'd press himself up against me and I'd lose control of everything. And I was terrified he'd move away, and apologize, and offer to drive me home. That was the last thing I wanted.

"Um." Rick turned away for a second, and I didn't realize how intense his gaze had been until he did. Then he locked eyes with me again, and it was even stronger. "Do you want to make out?"

"I-I might not be very good at it," I stuttered, swallowing. "I haven't done it much."

"I don't mind." Rick was looking at my mouth, and he swallowed too. "I want to kiss you. And this is the perfect spot for it: there's a view and—"

"Yeah, you brought me here on purpose, didn't you?"

Rick shrugged. "Maybe."

I reached my hand up to touch him. His neck, and then down over his shoulders and along his arm. He was so warm and strong. "Yeah, okay. You start."

So then he kissed me. And it was really, really nice. Better than that weird, anonymous kissing I'd done before. Turned out kissing was way better when you actually knew and liked the person. Well, for me, anyway. I really hadn't had that much experience, so it was plenty sloppy and awkward, especially considering we were in a vehicle. That is, until Rick leaned over to grab me and pull me onto his lap.

Seriously! I was straddling a guy, in his SUV, with a freaking sunset behind me, and making out with him, like all desperate and stuff. I couldn't even believe it. Not that I was thinking about that at the time. Or anything. Mostly I was thinking about how his mouth tasted, and how our bodies were all pressed together, and how his hands were totally roaming, like down my back and over my butt . . .

And then his hands went under my shirt, and he started sliding them up my back. For a moment I didn't care, because it felt so good on my bare skin, and like I said, I *really* wasn't thinking at that moment. But then I remembered my markings, and Captain Liberty telling me when I first started at the Legion: *"The fewer people who know the better. You never know how someone will react."* And really, thinking of Captain Liberty while kissing Rick was more than enough to make me feel all squicky and weird. And the little logical Javier in my head who was probably feeling a bit ignored through all of this was like: *You know, you've only been dating this guy for like three days. Are you gonna reveal your identity to all your three-day boyfriends? You whore.*

Apparently Logical-Javier was a jerky slut-shamer. Who knew?

So I stopped, made sure to pull my shirt back down, and sort of moved away. And then of course I bumped into the steering wheel with my butt and set off the horn, which made us both jump like a foot in the air. And then I saw the hurt, guilty expression on Rick's face.

"Oh no!" I stammered. "It's okay, that was okay!"

"It wasn't. I should have asked."

"I didn't mind it, really!" I didn't know how to explain without telling him the truth. "I liked it, it's just—"

"You want to—"

"I wanna wait."

"I understand."

"No." I sat back on the seat. "It's not for the reasons you think. I mean it's not like I haven't—"

"Because if you haven't, it's okay—"

"I have! It's just I need time . . ."

"For sure, I understand."

". . . before I can open up."

"Oh."

"Not like that!" I covered my face with my hands. "I mean, also like that, but . . . ugh." My face was burning, and my body was all angry with me, and I was all hot and desperate for air. "Maybe we should go for a walk."

"Good idea." Rick pulled his keys out of the ignition and opened the door, and I practically tumbled out the other side. "You want to take the path?"

"Yeah, that sounds good." I took some deep breaths, trying to bring my heart rate down before meeting Rick on the other side of the SUV.

So we went for a walk down the forest path, where we could see the city through the gaps in the trees, until the sun had set completely and the sky was black except for the few stars and the pinkish glow of the lights. A few moths fluttered around us, and bats flew overhead. Rick touched my waist and we stopped. He tugged me close and kissed me again, me up on my tiptoes to reach him, my arms around his neck.

I felt safe, excited, and like Rick was right: things were going to get better. But, of course, they had to get more complicated first. They always do.

CHAPTER THREE

The next night, during dinner, I got a call from Captain Liberty. My parents were always super big on the whole *dinner is a sit down together time* thing, especially since my mom worked evenings four nights a week, but they'd gotten a bit more lax about it since I'd gotten my job at the "pizza place." I almost didn't answer the phone, but my mom said it was okay. I think they liked that I was bringing in a bit of extra money, even though I mostly spent it all on myself.

I rushed into my room, half a slice of pita bread in my mouth, and shut the door before answering. "Hello?"

"Blue! Hello, are you alone?"

"Captain Liberty?" I said around a mouthful of bread. "What's up? I'm having dinner."

"I'm sorry to pull you away. I'm afraid there's been an unfortunate development. Do you remember Fritz Schneider, the man from the office you rescued the other day?"

"Yeah." I finished chewing and swallowed. "Is he all right?"

"We don't know. We'd put him with a guardian because we suspected the Organization might attempt to kidnap him in order to gain access to the safe they stole."

"Couldn't they just, like, break it open?"

"It's rigged to self-destruct if tampered with," said Captain Liberty. "I'm sure you've deduced by now that it contains valuable computer files."

"I did kind of, yeah. So, what, they managed to kidnap him?"

"Unfortunately, yes. Fortunately, we also placed a tracking chip in the safe itself, so we know where they might be holding him. It's vital that we recover the files before they are accessed, and of course, Mr. Schneider himself."

"Of course. So why are you telling me? You want me to do it?"

"Not exactly," said Captain Liberty. "It's a very crucial mission, but we don't want to risk starting an all-out war with the Organization, so I've decided to send one of my best stealth agents in. Her name is the Raven. She's excellent at reconnaissance, has a tremendous amount of fieldwork under her belt, but I've instructed her to pull out the moment things go south, and I have great confidence in her ability to do so safely."

I'd heard of the Raven. She was supposed to have fought in . . . um, a war. I can't remember which one—so sue me—and then defected to America, where she joined the Legion. There really wasn't much info about her besides that.

"I thought this might be a good opportunity for you," continued Captain Liberty, like he was just talking about some boring work experience. "We often send Junior Heroes alongside Senior ones on missions. Besides that, you are one of the very few people who has experience with these particular offenders, which can often prove very useful." When I didn't say anything for a moment, he went on. "Of course, there is a level of danger involved, so you can always refuse. Your status as a Junior Hero and a minor allows that."

Part of me did want to say *no way* and go back to dinner. But on the other hand, Captain Liberty had a good point, that I knew more about the baddies than anyone else, courtesy of having had the crap beaten out of me by them a couple of times. And I kind of wanted the chance to punch Jimmy Black in his big smug face. And, well, experience was good, right? If I ever wanted to be a proper Hero instead of just a Junior one, I'd have to start carrying out some more dangerous missions. "All right. When do you want me?"

"Tonight, if possible."

The Raven was terrifying. I'd seen her around the Legion before, but we'd never actually met. I'd kind of avoided her, honestly, mostly because I was afraid she'd crush me. She was like six feet of ripped muscles and sharp black feathery costume and buzzed silver hair. She was old too, like probably fifty, but I had no doubt she could beat the crap out of me. Apparently she had psychic powers (like the kind where you can move stuff around with your mind) and she could fly and summon, like, glowing energy or something. And she was not happy about me coming with her.

"You implied this was a rescue mission," she said angrily to Captain Liberty. Her accent could cut metal, I swear. "In and out. Now you want me to recover this safe also, *and* I will probably end up rescuing this boy along with Schneider."

"Blue can hold his own." Obviously Captain Liberty had a lot more confidence in me than I did. "He'll be an asset." He didn't say anything about the safe.

"I do not work with partners." The Raven glared at me past the sharp angles of her black mask. "You will do exactly as I say, understand?"

"Yes, ma'am," I squeaked. "What's the plan?"

"The safe, and likely Schneider also," said Captain Liberty with a quick glance at the Raven, "are located in a forty-story office building in the business sector." The Raven turned her sharp eyes away from me, which was a huge relief. We were in one of the Legion briefing rooms. It was all sleek and silvery with a big blue screen where a digital outline of the building was displayed. "You will be able to track the safe within five feet, but unfortunately the tracker doesn't include altitude, so we have no idea which floor it's on. You may need to search each floor. If you are attacked, or in any way compromised, you will withdraw immediately. We do not need another hostage on our hands. The Organization already has too many."

"Sir." The Raven shifted her weight from one foot to the other. "Is our primary objective the safe, or the hostage?"

"Ideally, you will be able to retrieve both."

"Yes. But primarily."

Captain Liberty sighed and put his hands on his hips. "I can't make that decision for you. But you know the consequences if we don't retrieve that data."

"This is a bad idea," said the Raven. "It would be safer to remove the chips."

Captain Liberty didn't say anything, and the Raven *tsk*ed and swept away. "Come, Blue Spark. Let's get ready."

The business sector was where all those tall, shiny buildings I'd mentioned were. I'd never really been near them because they give off a really strong *no poor people* vibe that I'm more than happy to obey. I consoled myself with thinking that no one knew Blue Spark was secretly a poor-as-dirt high schooler. I could go home to my penthouse every night, for all they knew.

The Raven could probably tell though. Not that she necessarily cared. Those are just the kind of things I think about to distract myself when I'm forty stories in the air and clinging to the back of a levitating Senior Hero.

The wind was cold and harsh this high up, whipping my hair around and freezing my ears. Below us, the streets and cars looked like a glowing miniature. I'm sure it was beautiful, but I felt like throwing up. I couldn't help imagining myself back home, warm in bed, with the sounds of the city muted and nonthreatening. Instead I was hanging by absolutely nothing, about a million feet up, and it was all I could do to keep from screaming.

I mean, don't get me wrong, part of me was excited too. But I was excited in a sort of anxious way. I wanted this to be over so that I could look back on it happily, instead of it happening right now, when I was absolutely terrified.

The Raven whipped out her little tablet and tapped it a few times. "The building's security system is disabled. We shouldn't have a problem getting in."

We moved closer, her gliding gracefully through the air, and me clinging to her back like some weird, terrified monkey. The building was huge up close, a big expanse of gleaming glass in every direction. The Raven put her hand on a pane and went to grab something in her belt. Then she stopped, turning her head to look at me. "Can you break this?"

"Uh, yeah." I shifted so I was higher up on her back and reached over her shoulder, placing my hand against the window and shooting a high-pitched sonic wave into the glass, shattering it inward.

"Excellent. Thank you."

We floated in, and I had to stop myself from falling to the floor and hugging the solid ground. The Raven alighted softly, the shattered glass crunching under her boots as she pulled out her tablet again, tapping away while sweeping the room with her dark eyes.

"Right. The scanner says the safe is in this location." She walked into an empty corner and stopped. "But obviously there is nothing here. We will go down."

"Okay," I replied. "How—"

"Hello," said a man's voice, and I nearly jumped out of my skin. The voice had an English accent, and it was tinny, like it was coming through a speaker, even though I couldn't see one anywhere. I couldn't tell which direction it was coming from at all; it was almost like he was speaking inside my skull. "I'm afraid you are trespassing on private property."

"I recognize this voice," said the Raven quietly to me. "His name is Williams, Organization head." Then she spoke up. "We are looking for Fritz Schneider. We believe he is being held here against his will."

"I'm afraid," said the voice again, "that you are trespassing on private property. We apologize for this inconvenience."

"What inconvenience?" I asked, although I was pretty sure I didn't really want to know.

There was a clicking noise, and before either of us could react, solid metal bars shot down all around us, trapping us. The Raven put her tablet in her belt and took a step toward them, reaching out . . .

Crack! There was a flash of red light, and she was thrown backward, red electricity sizzling through the air around her.

"Raven!" I ran to where she'd landed on her back, her head having narrowly missed impact with a desk. "Oh my god, are you okay?"

"Fine," she said, her teeth gritted. "I have no use for you if you are going to panic."

"I'm not panicking!" I insisted, although, okay, I was a bit. I mean, Captain Liberty had just thrown us in here willy-nilly, without much of a plan at all, and here we were trapped, and who knew what the Organization was going to do with us? Of course I was a little scared. "I'll be fine."

"Good." The Raven lifted her arm suddenly, and the ceiling above us crumbled and gave way. In what felt like less than a second, the Raven's arms were around me, and she was rushing up through the dust and debris, through a tear in plate metal, and into a large ventilation shaft. My feet barely touched the floor before she said, "Run."

I ran. Our feet pounded and echoed on the metal as we raced down the narrow shafts, dark but for the dim illumination through the occasional grate. I lost all track of where we were, but ahead of me, the Raven had pulled out her tablet, a little map on it glowing in the darkness.

Finally we stopped, and I doubled over to breathe. Okay, maybe I did need to spend a bit more time at the Legion gym.

"Are we lost?" I asked, and the Raven gave me an annoyed look.

"No. But we're moving away from the location of the safe. We need to go down."

"But," I panted, "shouldn't we get out of here?"

"What? Why?"

"Because—" *gasp, heave* "—the Organization, they know we're here. They trapped us."

The Raven *tsk*ed. "Please. No one traps me. When I am ready to leave, we will do so."

I straightened up and managed a little smile at her in the darkness. "You weren't scared back there?"

"The only thing I am afraid of right now is you panicking like a little rabbit and putting us both in danger." She tapped her tablet. "Panicking is the fastest way to doom yourself. If you stay calm, and rational, you can escape ninety-nine percent of hopeless situations. You understand?"

"Yeah." I nodded. I could do that. Right? "So what now?"

I gave a little yelp as the ground gave out from underneath us. I dropped a couple of inches, before bouncing back up and hopping in place. The Raven was floating in place too, seeming unfazed.

"Trapdoor," she said. "What is the easiest way to get into a prison?"

"You want to let them capture us?" It made sense, of course. But it was also terrifying. Not in the least because it meant we would have to fall to what could potentially be our doom. "And then we escape?"

"Exactly. Now, drop."

I did so, despite every atom in my body screaming at me not to. It was like all of my worst nightmares were finally realized. My gut churning, the wind whistling past my ears. For a second, I was back in that lightning storm, falling off an electrical wire to what I was sure was my death, with blue lightning cracking around me.

There was a burst of air from under us, slowing us down and buffeting me hard in the face, and then, finally, a light appeared. The Raven managed to catch herself before she hit the ground, but of course I landed with all the grace of a drunk bag of rocks. When I picked myself up, everything was bright and disturbingly . . . pastel.

For a moment I thought I must have hit my head. Like, surely this was some sort of weird, concussion-fueled hallucination. We were in what looked like an old lady's living room. Seriously, like floral-patterned furniture, bad pink carpet, kitschy Bible paintings on the wall. It was awful. And *weird*.

"Uh," I said softly. "Where the hell are we?"

The Raven glanced at me sideways. "I have no idea. Underground, I think."

There were no windows, and the place had a dim, sort of claustrophobic feel to it. The lights above us were buzzing fluorescents, and there was no sign of the trapdoor we'd obviously fallen through. I swallowed my rising panic and looked at the Raven, but she seemed momentarily stunned by the change of décor.

A little boxy TV on a wooden stand in the corner came to life suddenly, it's bulbous screen buzzing with static before an image of a thin man in a suit appeared.

"Hello." It was the same voice as the speaker upstairs. "I'm afraid that you are trespassing on private property. Please wait while we facilitate your arrival." The man disappeared, replaced by static, then reappeared. "Hello. I'm afraid that you are trespassing on private property. An attendant will be with you shortly. Please wait."

"We're . . . not going to wait, are we?" I asked.

The Raven went to one of the walls and placed her hands on it. "I don't want to use explosive force, it could trigger a collapse. But there must be a way in and out of here."

"Yeah, through the roof."

"We don't need to go up yet," she muttered. "Be careful what you say, they are probably watching us."

"Right," I said. The Raven continued to search for a hidden door, so I did the same, feeling up the wall with my hands, and then (in a stroke of genius, I think) my echolocation. I made my way around the room, until suddenly my echolocation came back different, and I waved the Raven over. "I think this is the door."

She gave me a rare proud expression. "Right. Stand back. Actually, why don't you do it?"

"Blast through the wall?" I stared up at her with my eyes big. "I don't know if I can."

"Nothing like the field to test your abilities." She stood back. "Go ahead."

I nodded and placed my hands on the floral wallpaper, pinpointing the door with little echolocation waves. Then I concentrated and sent a shock wave so hard that the Raven had to cover her ears. The door burst out, taking the wallpaper with it, and slid down the hallway ahead.

"Huh." The Raven stepped past me and out into the hallway. "Just like Tuvia."

"What did you say?" I rushed after her. "You worked with Tuvia? What were they like?"

"Stay focused on the mission, please."

The hallway was more of the same décor. I was beginning to think this must be some sort of weird mind-games thing. If that was the case, it was certainly doing its job. I felt squicked out, and I wanted desperately to get out of there.

We were at the end of the hallway, and on either side were more doors, these ones metal and sitting flush with the wall.

"I imagine our prisoner is in one of these." The Raven walked closer to examine one.

"This doesn't feel right," I said. "Shouldn't someone be attacking us by now?"

"Yes. So let's not waste time."

She handled the door this time, in a way that made it sort of implode on itself. With a glance around, she stepped into the room, her hands held up and glowing a threatening purple. I followed her warily.

It was another old-lady room, this one with a big four-poster bed against the wall. There was a man lying on it apparently asleep.

"It's not Fritz." The Raven went up to him and warily checked his vitals. "Hello, can you hear me?"

I leaned over just as the man's eyes snapped open. He flailed, trying and failing to hit the Raven, who caught his hand in hers. "Calm down. We're here to help you."

"Get away!" he screamed, his voice strange and unearthly. "It's a trick, it's another trick! I won't listen to you!"

"Shush!" said the Raven, but the man continued to flail and attack her. "Blue, can you please—"

I dived in to grab the man's kicking legs, but not before he landed a good one on my cheek. Rage automatically swelled up through me at the pain, even though I knew it was probably not the guy's fault.

"Damn it." She let go of the man's hands long enough to touch her fingers to his temple. He went limp.

"Great," I said. "Now what?"

The Raven grunted as she swung the man up over her shoulder. "Let's go."

Back into the hallway we went, the buzz from the fluorescent lights making my head feel numb, and the horrible wallpaper making my eyes hurt. The Raven pulled out her tablet again and frowned at it. "We're not in the right place."

"Should we be going after the safe first?" I asked, and she pursed her lips.

"No. Prisoners first. That door next, please."

I went and broke the next one down, blowing it off its hinges and into the room.

"What the hell?" said a man's voice from inside, and we rushed in. It was another floral room, but this one had what looked like a hospital bed, with a man lying, forcibly restrained on it. He lifted his head and looked at us. "Oh, thank god. This isn't a trick, is it?"

"Fritz." The Raven sounded relieved and annoyed at the same time. "What happened?"

"You've got to get out of here now," said Fritz, struggling as the Raven set her unconscious passenger down and went to Fritz's side. "It's bigger than that safe. If they get to you—"

"What do you mean, if they get to me?" she asked as she worked on breaking his restraints. "What are you talking about?"

"Ivana." Fritz sat up as she finished releasing his wrists, and gripped her forearm. "They have a Hound."

The Raven went stiff. "There are no Hounds in America."

"There's one here. I've seen her. She's been trying to get into my head. It's only a matter of time."

The Raven finished breaking Fritz's restraints, and he stood gingerly, favoring one of his legs.

"Blue, help him." The Raven picked up the unconscious man again, throwing him over her shoulder. "We're leaving."

"But what about the other prisoners?" I asked. "The safe?"

"*Now.*"

I rushed to Fritz's side and let him lean on me.

"Oh, I remember you," he said as we limped to the door. "Thank you for saving me."

"I didn't really." We hobbled through the door and came face-to-face with two Organization men in black suits, followed by a short old woman with curly gray hair and a floral dress.

"Oh!" she said pleasantly. "Why, hello there."

The man over the Raven's shoulder woke up suddenly and started jerking his body around. The Raven did her best to fight him, but he dragged his nails over her face before she could stop him, drawing blood. And then he went at her neck, like a freaking vampire, and when she threw him off, he came rushing back at her. She could probably take him no problem normally, but he was berserk, like rabid. It was terrifying, and of course while I was staring, one of the Organization guys rammed right into me, sending Fritz toppling to the floor and me flying into the wall.

I got up, doing my best to ignore that the wind had been knocked out of me, and rushed him, shoving him back into the other guy, who was going for the Raven. The first guy turned just in time and grabbed me by the throat, while the other one slammed his fist into my stomach. I saw stars for a moment, and then there was a flash of purple and a *whumph* as one of the guys was thrown away from me. The Raven's hand was in the hair of the guy holding me, dragging his head backward while she brought a hand to his throat, incapacitating him with her powers. He dropped to the ground instantly.

"I said we are leaving," she growled. "We are *leaving*."

The last thing I saw was that creepy old lady coming at me, her face all distorted like some kind of animal, and her eyes pitch-black. Then there was this wall of purple fire around us, shooting up from the ground, and my stomach was doing somersaults that made that fall earlier feel like a nice day on the beach.

Then the fire burned down, and I dropped to my knees and puked, all over the Legion's nice shiny metal floor.

"What happened?" Captain Liberty was there, rushing forward. He was waylaid by the berserk guy, who jumped him with an unearthly scream. The Raven moved quickly, pulling him off Captain Liberty and knocking him out again so that he slumped to the floor.

I managed to lift my head a little and look around. There were three people on the floor besides me. Fritz, who had fallen over and was clutching his leg, crazy scratchy guy, and the Organization guy who had been trying to choke me to death. He was properly passed out as well.

"What just happened?" I still felt like my stomach was trying to turn itself inside out. "How did we get here?"

"I teleported," said the Raven gruffly. "Fail-safe. Now I need to go sit down."

Along with feeling nauseous, I was also kind of confused and angry. Why hadn't Captain Liberty or the Raven told me that we could have teleported out of there at any time? They'd let me freak out and think we were going to be captured. I almost wanted to yell at the two of them, but they were already glaring at each other, and I didn't want them redirecting their wrath at me.

"What," said Captain Liberty again, deadly serious, "happened?"

The Raven really did look exhausted, and definitely not in the mood to be interrogated. "You want to know what happened? *You* sent both of us in there unprepared. You should have done your research! There was a Hound there."

"A Hound?" Captain Liberty's face went white. "Are you sure?"

"Yes, I am damn well sure. Ask *him*." The Raven gestured at the man on the floor. On closer inspection, he didn't look too good. His hair was gray and thinning, he had a scruffy beard, and his body was thin. Way too thin. "What do you think she did to him?"

"What in the hell is going on?"

Oh great. The Wolfhound. He and Lady Deathquake strode into the room, along with a bunch of other people, all of whom got to see me kneeling on the ground in my own puke. *Great.* This was worse than the bug thing.

The Raven straightened up. "He—" she pointed viciously at Captain Liberty "—is so desperate to get his bloody chip technology back, he almost sent us to our deaths. Or worse."

Captain Liberty seemed remarkably unoffended. "Did you retrieve the safe?"

The Raven's nostrils flared. "No."

"It's my fault," said Fritz from the floor. "It's my fault it got stolen in the first place."

"It's not your fault!" I said, turning to him.

"Blue, are you all right?" That was Lady Deathquake, coming to kneel next to me. She put an arm around my shoulders and helped me up. She smelled nice, and even with her mask on I could tell she was really pretty. I wondered why she was with a loser like Wolfhound.

"I'm okay," I said, more to reassure her than anything, because I really, really wasn't okay.

Captain Liberty looked like he was thinking hard. "I can see that I've made several mistakes today."

"Finally you're talking sense," spat the Wolfhound.

"I'm sorry I was desperate to retrieve the technology," Captain Liberty continued, ignoring Wolfhound and turning to the Raven. "I put you and Blue in danger because of my own stubbornness."

"It's not *that* bad," I said. This was all a little unfair to the captain. But he was going along with it.

"And I'm sorry to you too, Blue." He turned to me. "I treated this like a training mission when it was obviously something more serious than that. I didn't brief you fully, and I'll understand if I've lost your trust."

"Who cares about him?" The Wolfhound snorted. "If you can't guarantee that the Organization doesn't have access to that technology, then I want this damn chip out of me right now."

"Fritz," said the Raven. "Did you tell him the pass code?"

"I don't think so," said Fritz. "But I—I don't know, she might have gotten into my head and made me forget about it. I don't know anything, really."

"Wait." I went over to one of the sleek silver chairs and collapsed into it. "Who is she? What's a Hound?"

"A psychic," said Lady Deathquake quietly. "A very powerful one, able to brainwash and manipulate people's minds."

"They look human." The Raven ground her teeth. "But they're not. At least not anymore."

Captain Liberty nodded stiffly. "If the Organization has a Hound on their side, they could be amassing an army. We need to be prepared for this."

"And we can start by not making it easy for them to track down every single one of us," said the Wolfhound. "Chips. Out. Now."

"You can elect to have yours removed at any time," said Captain Liberty. "But they are a valuable resource, and the decision to have the program discontinued would have to be put to a vote."

The Wolfhound took a menacing step toward the captain. "And while we're voting, they'll get into that safe—"

"We will attempt to retrieve the safe again," said Captain Liberty, standing his ground. "Within a couple of days, at the latest. Now that we know what we're dealing with, I'll put together an appropriate team for the situation."

"There is no appropriate way of dealing with a Hound," said the Raven darkly. "This will not end well."

So Fritz and the poor brainwashed guy went to be treated by the resident psychic. All I wanted to do was go home and sleep, but I had to give a detailed statement about everything that had gone down first, and then I had to trundle over to the psychic's office so she could check that *I* hadn't been brainwashed. She took the opportunity to ask me how I was feeling. I wanted to say that I was scared, and kind of freaked out, and that Captain Liberty's decision to not "brief me fully" had left a really bad taste in my mouth, even if he had apologized. I didn't know how to verbalize all that at the time though, so I just said, "Tired."

"Well, maybe you can come back in a couple of days when you're rested up." The psychic's name was Chelsea, and she was actually really nice. She had brown skin and big natural hair, and she sat with her stocking feet sideways on her couch across from me, which I thought was kind of cool. "I'm actually a registered therapist too, and the service is free for you."

"Yeah," I said. "Maybe. I'm not really into getting my mind read though."

"I don't read or tamper with anyone's mind, not without their explicit permission."

"Oh." That was a bit of a relief. "Well, maybe, but for now I should get home. I'm not, you know, brainwashed, am I?"

"No. I'd be able to tell."

"So . . ." I tilted my head. "What's the difference between you and a Hound, then?"

"I can't control people." She shook her head. "All I can do is read what they're thinking, momentarily confuse them. But Hounds . . . well, they can change a person's mind. Make them really believe something, make them loyal, even when the Hound isn't there physically to manipulate them. Also, I was born with my powers. Hounds are made."

"How?"

"Well . . ." She shifted and brought her feet up under her. "It is possible for even low-level psychics to break into someone's mind, if they have enough time, although it usually also breaks the person. Hounds are . . . created, I suppose, when a person resists that initial break-in. Something in them changes, they become less than human. Or more, I suppose, depending on how you look at it. They're very dangerous, and also very rare." She sighed. "I don't know how the Organization ended up with one working for them, but it's worrying. It means we can't trust anyone." She turned away, forcing a small smile. "I suppose this means I'll be getting a lot of work in the near future."

"I'm sure it'll be okay," I said. "I mean, you can remove the brainwashing, right?"

"Yes. But only if they consent to it. I wouldn't feel comfortable doing it otherwise."

"Right," I said. "Morals and everything."

"Something has to separate us from the Organization," she replied. "I can see you're tired. Why don't you head home?"

"Yeah." I stifled a yawn. "Okay."

I didn't realize that it was four in the morning until I changed into my street clothes in the alley outside our apartment and pulled out my cell phone to check my messages There were ten missed calls from my parents, and when I got upstairs and went inside, they were sitting on the couch, still fully dressed.

My stomach sank down into my shoes. "Um. H-hola. You guys are still up."

"It's four in the morning," said my mother. "Where were you?"

"I got called into work, remember?"

"Until four."

"We had . . . cleaning."

"No Pizza Hut in town is open past one," said my father. "Javier, where were you?"

"I . . . just . . . out."

"Were you with your boyfriend?" asked my mother. "Because it's okay if you were, but we expect you to tell us."

"No, I wasn't with him."

"Then where?" said my father. "Javier, you understand, we give you a lot of freedom, but in return we expect you to be honest with us."

They were both sitting there staring at me, looking upset, with their faces all lined, and I wanted so badly to just tell them. But I was so tired, and everything hurt, and I knew that there was a chip in my butt that could potentially lead a bunch of Organization people right to them, and that made me feel guilty, and worried, and *scared*. Some really scary stuff had gone down, and was going down, and I wasn't ready . . . I wasn't ready to talk about it with anyone. None of it.

"I'm almost eighteen," I said. "I can do what I want."

I hated myself as soon as I said it. It was awful, and I expected them to go off on me like they had when I'd left the fridge open overnight, or banged a hole in the bathroom wall. But instead my father just said, "Fine. Go to bed. We'll talk about it later." Which was, like, ten times worse.

I slunk into my room and slammed the door. I kind of wanted to cry, but I was still too strung out for that. I couldn't even remember the last time I'd cried. Maybe I couldn't anymore. I slid my bag off and collapsed onto the bed, curling up on my side still fully clothed. I didn't see much point in sleeping, since I'd have to get up in like three hours to go to school. I definitely wasn't skipping, not after my parents were already so upset. I could feel myself drifting off though, so I reached down to grab my phone and set my alarm.

With all the calls from my parents, I'd missed a text from Rick. *Hey Javier. Lunch tomorrow?*

I smiled, and the next thing I knew, my alarm was going off somewhere on the floor, and sunlight was streaming through my dingy curtains.

I slept in my contacts by the way. Fantastic. And it wasn't as if I could just take a break from wearing them, since people would probably notice if I was in class with glowing blue eyes. Instead I just brought my bottle of saline with me and went to the bathroom between classes to shoot it into my eyes. Between that and the three hours of sleep, I was surprised Rick didn't think I was high when we met at the mall food court for lunch. He did ask if I was okay, which was nice.

I shrugged. "Yeah, I just worked late."

"Oh, do you work tomorrow? I was just wondering if you wanted to come to my place after school. My dad's on a business trip, and my mom's taking my sister to some cadet thing, so we'd have the place to ourselves."

"Oh." I blinked at him. "I don't know."

"I mean—" Rick looked chagrined. "We don't have to . . . We could do anything. We could, like, watch a movie or go swimming or something."

"No, it's not that— Wait, you have a pool?"

"Uh, yeah. Why?"

I shook my head. "No way, I can't."

"We don't have to go swimming."

"No, I can't . . ." I took a sip of my pop. "I can't go to your house, I'd feel weird."

"Well, okay, but . . . why?"

"Because." I waved my arms. "You've seen where I live. The only reason someone like me would end up in your parent's pool is if I was cleaning it."

Rick laughed out loud. "Come on, Javier. My parents aren't like that."

"Really? Who do they get to clean the pool?"

"Uh . . . some guy."

I raised my eyebrows at him. "What's his name?"

"Felipe—you're being unfair!"

"Uh-huh." I took another sip of my drink. "Have you told your parents you're dating a pool boy?"

"You're not a pool boy!" Rick was almost out of his chair in agitation. "Javier . . ."

"Calm down, I'm just messing with you. Anyway, what's wrong with being a pool boy?"

"I'm beginning to see why you're friends with Kendall." He sat back down.

"What do you mean by that?"

"No way." Rick threw his hands up, but he was laughing. "I'm not saying anything else."

I grinned at him. "I'll come to your house. But I'm not swimming."

"Never said you had to swim."

"What movies do you have?"

"What movies do you *like*?"

So that was how I ended up at Rick's place after school the next day. And it was even worse than I'd imagined. And by worse I mean *huge*. It looked, no lie, like the freaking White House. With big pillars on either side of the door, and big rectangular windows, and the front yard all manicured.

And then we walked in the front door, and I resolved right then and there that I was never, ever, *ever* letting Rick see my apartment. Not even if we ended up getting married and spending the rest of our lives together. And it was no shade on my parents or anything, it was just . . . this place, it was from another world. You walked in the front door and the floors were all light hardwood, and the ceiling went up two stories and there was a big winding staircase in front of us. I kid you not. A *winding staircase*. With dripping crystal chandelier stuff hanging from the ceiling. The whole place felt all airy and peaceful, and kind of museum-ish.

I stood there gawking like an idiot while Rick took my coat, and then he led me up the stairs and down a big hallway into his bedroom.

You know how they say you can tell a lot about a person from their bedroom? That was so totally true of Rick. He had a big shelf with awards and framed photos, and one of those triangular cloth things with the school logo on it on the wall. I don't know what they're called, okay? And then a bunch of pictures of football players, and an entertainment stand with a flat-screen TV and a huge collection of movies and video games, and of course, a desk with a shiny new iMac. And his room was, like, clean. All neat and tidy with his bed made and everything in its place. As opposed to my room, where the bed was never made, it was a miracle if you could see the floor, and my closet was perpetually open with every single thing I've ever acquired since I was six spilling out of it. Rick's closet was closed, and I bet if you opened it, there'd be shelves with his shoes and stuff all neatly lined up on them. Because that was Rick.

I went to the window and gazed out over the big, fenced backyard and the picture-perfect suburbia beyond. They did have a pool, and for a moment I wished we could go swimming in it. I imagined waiting until the nighttime and skinny-dipping with Rick, the glow from my skin lighting up the pool while we pressed our bodies together . . .

I cleared my throat and turned around. Rick was standing in the doorway, looking nervous.

"It's really nice," I said. "Seriously, your house is beautiful."

"I know," he said, a little sheepishly. "I never thought about it before. I kind of want to see your place now."

I smirked and shook my head. "Nooo, you don't."

"I do. I bet it's got personality."

"Ha!" I laughed and went over to the TV stand. "You weren't lying, you do have every single season of *Star Trek* on DVD."

"I can't believe you don't like sci-fi!"

"We live in a city where hundreds of people got superpowers when a chemical reactor exploded. That's not sci-fi enough for you?"

Rick surprised me by coming up behind me and grabbing me around the waist. "Okay, so what do you like? You said . . . Westerns?"

"Do you have any?"

"I have an episode of *Star Trek* set in the old west."

"No, come on."

"I don't!" Rick kissed the side of my neck, sending shivers down my body. "I bet there's something on Netflix though."

"I've seen all the Westerns on Netflix."

He kissed my neck again, and then up under my ear. "So show them to me."

"Fine." I giggled. "Fine, but you have to stop that!"

"Mmm. Okay." He didn't stop. I think he could tell I didn't want him to. Instead his hands roamed around my waist and up over my stomach.

"Rick. Seriously." I leaned back and tilted my head sideways to kiss him.

"Sorry!" He pulled away and ducked around me to turn on the TV. "I'm terrible. Honestly, just smack me if I try to go too far."

"It's fine." I was doing my very best not to melt into the floor. "You'll know if I want you to stop."

Rick went and lay on the bed, propping some pillows up and grabbing the controller. "Okay, Westerns . . ."

I crawled onto the bed next to him. He chose a Clint Eastwood movie and clapped to turn the light off.

I'd seen this one like a million times with my dad, but I got into it anyway, relaxing on Rick's comfortable bed and leaning on his shoulder. Everything was going great, until at a particularly exciting part, I glanced over and realized that Rick wasn't watching the movie; he was looking at me.

"You're not even paying attention!" I yelled, swatting him with a pillow.

"Hey, sorry!" He ducked out of the way. "Sorry, ow! You distracted me!"

"I'm just sitting here all slouched! How is that distracting?"

"You're so into it." Rick hunched his shoulders defensively. "It's really cute. Sometimes you mouth the lines."

I buried my face in the pillow, knocking my glasses askew. "Oh my god, that's so embarrassing!" I lifted my head out of the pillow so I could glare at him.

"I'm sorry." He gave me a lopsided grin. "I didn't mean to embarrass you. You're just really pretty. I like looking at you. And . . ." His face became apologetic. "It's a really boring movie."

"It's an awesome movie! It's quintessential! Cinematic! You just can't appreciate it."

"I know, I know!" Rick put his hands up in defeat. "How'd you get into them anyway?"

I rolled my head. "My dad. He *loves* them. When we first moved to America, I thought it was gonna be like the Wild West, and I was so excited."

"Not so much?" Rick grinned again

"Not at all." I pouted. "And there's just, you know, something about them. They're simple. You know who the bad guys are."

"Yeah, that's what I *don't* like about them." Rick leaned back on the pillows. "Real life isn't that simple."

"No, but the rules still apply. If you hurt people for personal gain, you're a bad person."

"Sure but how do you know what someone's motivation is? You can't. I don't know. I *used* to agree with you."

"So what changed?"

"I don't know." Rick jerked his shoulder into a shrug. "I grew up, I guess. After that accident, it's like . . . things got more complicated. Morality didn't seem so black-and-white anymore. Like, take the Legion, for example. We grow up being told that superheroes are the good guys, right? We get it force-fed down our throat. But what if that's not the truth?"

"It is though." I felt a bit of nerves and unhappiness in the pit of my stomach. "They help people."

"Yeah, sure, to keep their public image good. I mean, who knows what kind of agenda they've got going on underneath."

"I don't think—"

"Yeah, but you don't *know*," said Rick. "I don't know. It just makes me feel . . . I don't know." He sank down onto the bed. Despite being a little annoyed at him for dissing the Legion, I wanted to make him feel better. I brushed a piece of black hair out of his eyes and leaned tentatively up against him again. "You okay?"

"Yeah." He sighed. "I'm sorry. I guess that car crash really messed me up."

"It would anyone," I said, trying to reassure him, even though I didn't really know if anything would help.

"I feel . . ." He grabbed my hand, playing with my fingers. "I feel like there's this darkness inside of me, you know?" He squeezed my hand and let it go. "Sorry, that's a weird thing to say."

"No." I looked up at him. "I feel that way sometimes too. I think everyone does."

"Or maybe we're both just messed up."

"Maybe." I put my cheek back down on his chest. "I think you're a good guy, Rick."

"Thanks." He slid an arm around me. "You too."

I craned my head up to kiss him, and then rolled over so I was lying on him, our bodies pressed together. His hands moved down my back again, but didn't go under my shirt this time. I could feel myself getting . . . well, you know, and I wondered if maybe we should stop.

If it weren't for what he'd said about the Legion, I'd probably have just told him right then and there. I didn't know what to do, but I knew I didn't want to stop kissing him.

Our phones started ringing at the same time. Which later I thought was weird, but at the time I didn't even notice because I was a bit, um, distracted. The contrasting melodies were pretty annoying though, so we sort of awkwardly detangled ourselves and went to answer them.

It was a call from the Legion. I picked up, and with a nervous glance at Rick, darted out into the hall.

"Yeah?"

"Blue Spark? This is Beth, at the Legion dispatch, requesting all hero support to the business sector."

"What?" I held my hand up to my mouth and whispered. "What's going on?"

"There's really no time to explain in detail, but we need help evacuating civilians. How soon can you be here?"

The bedroom door opened, and Rick barreled out past me. He turned to look at me, eyes wide, as if he'd forgotten I was there. "Sorry, uh, Javier." He was clutching a backpack to his chest. "I, uh, gotta go to work. Emergency."

"Yeah." I nodded. "Me too, could you drive me?"

He swallowed. "Yeah, sure. Downtown?"

"Uh-huh. You could just drop me off."

"Okay."

"Okay."

I brought the phone up to my ear. "Maybe ten minutes?"

"Affirmative. As quick as you can, please." The line went dead.

Rick was already striding away, and I ran after him, down the spiral staircase and out the front door, which he locked hurriedly. The radio was on in his car, an emergency news broadcast playing.

"Civilians are being asked to stay clear of the business sector, while evacuation efforts are underway from Pine Street to South Delta. Initial assessments report damage to three buildings, and several vehicles and streets, as what appears to be an all-out battle between the Legion of Liberty and the Organization continues."

I gripped the side of the seat, jerking forward so fast that my seat belt locked. "What?"

Rick swore. "Well, what'd I tell you?"

"I wonder what happened," I said quietly, and Rick looked out the window. He was driving fast.

"Sources are unclear as to what incited the incident," the reporter went on. "After over two decades of relative peace, the tyrannical rule of the Organization over Liberty City is a distant memory to many. Could this battle hint to a possible return of those frightening days—"

Rick scoffed and turned the radio off.

"It's probably nothing." I swallowed. "They just like to sensationalize."

"They like to make people panic and hate the Organization."

"Um." I turned to him. "What's not to hate about the Organization? Do you know some of the stuff they did to people in the eighties?"

"Yeah, sure. I don't want to talk about it, we'll probably just disagree."

"Probably." I thumped back in my seat. "You can drop me off up here. I'll get the train."

The train only went like halfway there, of course, because evacuation, and then I had to do the whole running-and-jumping-along-rooftops thing, which I'm sure you know by now is my absolute favorite.

When I got there, it was like a disaster zone. The big shiny building we'd been in the other night was up in flames, big chunks missing from it, and black smoke billowing out of the holes. The pavement had huge craters in some places, and was buckled like there'd been an earthquake in others. Cars were toppled over and burning, windows were smashed, alarms were going off, and everywhere you looked there were superheroes and villains, all frantically battling it out like Smash Brothers. Only, you know, actually super dangerous and generally not at all like an enjoyable classic video game. Forget that reference.

There were civilians around too, huddled behind cars and inside store fronts, and I guessed that was where I came in. Most of the heroes were too distracted by villains to be able to do much except try to direct the damage away from civilians. Part of me wanted to help them, but Junior Heroes were technically not supposed to get into fights with the Organization, and they'd called me here specifically to help with evacuations.

And anyway, that was what superheroes were *supposed* to do, right? Help people.

I dropped down to a café with a bunch of people inside and started herding them out, introducing myself as I did so, and trying to reassure several old men who didn't seem to want to listen to me. My phone dinged, letting me know that there was an evacuation vehicle around the corner. I led them all along the smashed-up sidewalk, helping them over a particularly large crater at one point, and jumping in the air to catch a falling billboard at another. I'd probably be feeling that in my shoulders for months.

I got them to the transport vehicle, a city bus driven by a very determined-looking old woman. Once they were on, she announced that she couldn't hold any more and shut the door, driving off along the narrow strip of the road that was still intact. I turned around to see if there was anyone else I could help, and that's when I saw him.

Jimmy Black. Of course. He was, well, there was no other word for it. *Skulking.* Up to no good. I watched him pass by a hero and villain beating the crap out of each other, and then sneakily followed after him. Okay, well, maybe not quite as sneakily as I thought, because he turned right around and met my eyes, and then ran off.

"Hey!" I yelled. "Come back here! What are you up to?"

He ignored me, dodging into a McDonald's. I followed him, determined.

"Hey!" I shouted at him again, throwing the door open. "Jimmy Black, I'm talking to you!"

He ignored me and sauntered lazily up to the counter. "Can I get some service here?" He rapped on the table. The few staff members that were still present gave both of us horrified stares and skittered away out the back door. Jimmy watched them go, and then peered over the counter. "Hello? I want to order a burger!"

"What the hell are you doing?" I gaped at him.

He glared at me. "Ordering a burger, what's it look like?"

I glared right back. "You're up to something. I know it."

He shrugged. "Think what you want." He left the counter and headed toward the back of the restaurant. I followed him, a few paces behind, and he turned to face me. Even with his arms spread, and his posture relaxed, I didn't trust him. He was so much bigger than me, and so much darker. Looking at him was like trying to see in a room that was pitch-black. "I'm just going to the bathroom. Nothing to see."

"Ha-ha." I followed him into the bathroom, glancing around as we entered. There was no other exit, just a tiny window that I might have been able to wriggle out of, but he certainly wasn't going through.

He pulled a face at me, and went into one of the stalls, slamming it shut behind him.

I still wasn't sure what his game was, but I wasn't leaving him alone to get away. Not this time. I went to the mirror and examined my reflection, keeping an eye on the closed stall door as well. There was no sound from inside. I leaned forward, fixed my hair, straightened my mask. The stall door swung open, and I went to turn, but he was too quick.

From behind me, his hand gripped the back of my head and smashed it forward. My face impacted the glass, pain shooting through my entire body from my forehead. I saw white. The glass shattered, and I thought a few pieces of it got embedded in my scalp, although my mask took the brunt of it. I wheezed and slid to the floor, barely managing to avoid knocking my head on the sink.

For a moment my vision went black, and I wanted to just lie there on the floor and go to sleep. But then I saw Jimmy's boots step past me out the door, and I knew that nothing, not even the throbbing pain in my head or the possibility that I might have a deadly concussion, was worse than letting him get away.

I jumped up, ignoring the way my head swished like a goldfish bowl on a boat in the middle of a storm, and limped after him as he pulled the glass doors open and strode out into the street. It was quieter now, only a few sirens and the sound of burning in the distance. Jimmy was walking away, obviously unaware that I was still following him.

I changed that by leaping onto him and clawing at his face. Somewhere in my brain, I remembered that scratching in fighting wasn't really acceptable, but damn it, I was *angry* and I didn't care. I dug my fingers into his neck, hoping he could feel my nails through my gloves. He screamed and reached back, grabbing at me and spinning in circles. Finally he grabbed me by the arm, pulling me over his shoulder. I had to let go or risk my arm getting dislocated, not that I cared much at that moment, and he threw me forward, smashing me into the wall.

I was quick and managed to bounce off it, swinging my fist up and knocking him good in the face. He swore and brought a hand to his nose, which was bleeding profusely. Good, I hoped I'd broken it.

He swung at me, and I dodged out of the way, but he grabbed my wrist and pulled me forward, boxing me hard in the ear.

I slammed my hands into him, forcing him backward into a wall. He fell face-first into the ground, and I advanced on him, my fists clenched as he struggled to get up. I lifted my palms, unsure of what I was going to do to him, but angry enough that if I'd been in my right mind, I probably would have been terrified of myself. All I could think about was that darkness I'd mentioned to Rick, and how right then it was filling me to the brim.

He lunged at me, grabbing at my feet and knocking me off-balance. I rolled out of the way in time to avoid a punch aimed down at my head. It broke the concrete under me. I jumped at him, on impulse cupping my hands to his ears and sending a high-pitched whistle directly into them.

It worked better than I'd expected. His face contorted in pain, and he screamed, falling to his knees and reaching up to grab my hands. I slapped him away and put my hands to his ears again, doubling my efforts, focusing on his eardrums. He was gritting his teeth, his eyes clenched shut, his whole body vibrating in pain, but I didn't want to stop. His fingers found their way around my neck, but I was winning. If I could just knock him out first, before the blackness in my vision overcame me, if I could just get a breath between his thick fingers, hard as steel and clenching down on my throat . . .

My vision spotted and went black again. The high-pitched whistle was in my ears too, ringing like bells on a planet I'd never visited but knew anyway. I didn't feel my body going limp, but when the darkness overtook me, I felt weightless in a way I never had when I was falling. If only I could fly, then I wouldn't be so afraid of it, after all. If only I could sleep . . .

PART TWO

CHAPTER FOUR

So. You're probably wondering right now why everything in Liberty City is called dumb, patriotic names like Freedom Hill and Justice Park, et cetera. Oh, you weren't? Huh. Well, things got a little hot and heavy back there, so I think I'm going to take a break and tell you anyway.

The truth is, Liberty City started out as Valley City. I know, brilliant, right? And Freedom Hill was Pine Hill, and pretty much everything had boring names like that. And then in the forties, the Kingston Power Plant malfunctioned and exploded, and a bunch of people in the city started developing weird abilities. Some of them decided that they would use them to help people, and after a few years, they formed the Legion of Liberty, a group of superheroes led by Captain Liberty, who fought crime and watched over the city.

But, as it turns out, not everyone who gets superpowers wants to use them for good, and after a while, a group of superpowered villains called the Organization emerged. Naturally, they didn't exactly get along with the Legion. Civilians had to be careful because they never knew when a battle was going to break out and people might be in danger. But nothing really terrible happened until 1982. That's when the Organization successfully stormed the Legion headquarters and managed to drive the Legion and the government of Valley City out entirely.

Seriously, no one could do anything. Not the police, not the military, no one. For seven whole years, Valley City just *belonged* to the Organization. They ran the place. The people who could, left, but a lot of people had jobs and lives and families here, so they couldn't just up and leave. The Captain Liberty at the time knew they had to do something, so he convinced all the Legion members to band together to take the city back. There was a huge battle, and a lot of people died, but at the end of it, the city was reclaimed. To celebrate, they renamed it Liberty City, and gave everything else Legion-themed, patriotic names. Dumb, right? But there you have it.

Anyway, the reason I'm mentioning this is because after I woke up from my fight with Jimmy Black, the city looked like it did in the pictures in my history textbooks from after that big battle in 1989. And that was really damn scary.

The Raven had found me passed out on the cracked cement outside the McDonald's with my mask lying next to me. Jimmy Black was nowhere to be seen.

"He took my mask off," I said again, for what was probably the fifth time, as the Legion doctors examined me for a concussion and injuries. "Why would he do that?"

The Raven had stayed with me the entire way to the Legion headquarters, and was now hanging around to make sure that I was okay, which I was actually pretty grateful for.

"I'm not going to say that it's not a little worrying," she said. "But I don't think the Organization will let him do anything to compromise your identity. If they did, the Legion could consider it a breach of the arrangement, and arrest the Organization members whose identities *we* know. They don't want us to do that. So."

She walked over to stand in front of us and glanced at the nurse, who finished checking me out.

"You're fine," said the nurse. "You have a minor concussion, and you passed out from lack of air to your brain. I was a little worried about swelling around your airway, but it looks like the bruising on your neck has already started to heal, so I'd say the worst is behind you. Come in right away if you have any trouble breathing, but other than that, you're good to go."

I didn't exactly feel "good to go"—superhealing powers don't extend to emotional recovery unfortunately—but I didn't say anything, just nodded and hopped off the table to let the next person be examined.

"Come on," said the Raven. "There's an assembly, and Captain Liberty is going to let us all know what the hell just happened."

The assembly itself was pretty darn boring, so I'll summarize. Basically Captain Liberty spilled his guts about how the Organization had stolen the information about the chips, and how the attack on their headquarters had been a last-ditch attempt to get the information back. What he hadn't expected (and probably should have, he admitted, given what we now knew about the presence of a Hound at the Organization—that brought a gasp and a bunch more questions, of course) was for the Organization's forces to be so many or so strong, or for them to respond to the mission so violently.

So then they put it to a vote about whether or not we should remove the tracking chips and, since they'd been unsuccessful in retrieving the stolen information, almost unanimously decided that we should. They also decided that we all needed to get extra training so that we could be prepared in case the Organization tried to attack us, and Captain Liberty promised to put together a special task force to investigate and see if anything could be done about the Hound.

The scariest thing, for me, and I think for a lot of other people, was that some of the heroes had recognized a few of the villains they were fighting—they were former superheroes, ones who had mysteriously disappeared or been captured by the Organization and kept prisoner. And now they were fighting with the Organization, which, I mean, I guess that happens sometimes. But this time it was pretty obvious it was because they'd been brainwashed, and that made everyone feel really squicked out and afraid.

Captain Liberty also apologized for his lack of transparency, and promised to be more honest about everything that was going on. Apparently there needed to be some kind of reform in the way decisions were made, according to the Wolfhound anyway, and he and a few other senior heroes stayed in the assembly room debating things long after the majority of us had left.

I didn't really want to go home. It was getting dark, and I'd texted my parents that I'd been called into work, but I knew they'd be expecting me home soon. I stayed in my costume and went to one of the older areas of town. There was a cathedral there, and I climbed up it to sit on one of the spires and cry.

It wasn't that I was sad, really. It was . . . I didn't know, it wasn't really an emotion I'd felt before, so I didn't know how to describe it.

The closest I could come was the way I'd felt the first couple of weeks of school in America, when I couldn't speak English, and everything around me had been strange, confusing, and wrong. I'd just wanted everything to go back to the way it was before, even though I'd known that it wasn't going to, and even if it did, something would still be different. I'd cried then too, but then I'd had to do it where people could see me. Now I was alone, and staring at a sunset over the city that I'd come to feel was my home, and I was scared for it.

And I was scared for me.

Everyone else seemed like they had everything together, you know? Like even when they were sad, or angry, or hurt, they still knew what was going on. They still knew what they were doing with their life, and who they were.

Me? I had no idea. And I felt like I was the only one who didn't. Except maybe Rick, and I didn't even know what was going on with us right now. I wanted to see him, but I'd texted him and he hadn't replied, so I assumed he was still at work. But he'd seemed so annoyed at me earlier, and I didn't really know why.

I sighed and lay back, letting my stomach do little flops as I balanced precariously over nothing. I didn't like the anger I'd felt today. I didn't want it to be part of me. It didn't feel heroic. I certainly wasn't a fantastic hero, not by any stretch of the imagination, but I could damn well try. And I could start by never letting myself give in to anger the way I had today.

It made me felt better, having decided that. Like at least I was in control of some small aspect of my life. There was something I wanted to be like, or be *not* like, at least. And that was something.

I jumped off the side of the church and bounced down to the little building by the gardens, hiding behind it to change back into my street clothes. Then I took the bus home. I guess I didn't realize how bad I looked until my mom saw me and screamed. Turned out I had a black eye from the mirror thing. And I hadn't come up with any excuse ahead of time, so I ended up telling her that I'd "fallen into a glass display."

She hugged me. "Oh Javi, maybe you should consider getting a job that's better suited to someone as accident-prone as you, hmm?"

I had to admit it felt nice to have her dote on me a bit, and I was glad she didn't seem to be angry anymore about the other night.

I also had a little knot of worry at the bottom of my stomach, because Jimmy Black had seen my face. And he hadn't done it accidentally either. He'd taken my mask off, and looked at me. And if he'd found out who I was, and tried to take advantage of my parents, well . . . that dark rage inside of me that I'd decided to try to work on eliminating? I didn't think I'd have any chance at all of reining it in.

Rick wasn't at school the next day.

I know, I *know*, you don't have to say it. I'm an idiot.

But honestly, amidst all the strange and unlikely claims I have made about myself and my life over the course of this story, have I ever once given the impression that I am not, in fact, an idiot?

No? Then let's move on.

I texted him a couple of times. Not like, excessively. I didn't want to be creepy. But a couple of times. And then after school I called him, but he didn't pick up. I left a message saying that I hoped he was okay, and then went to Kendall's place for the afternoon, trying to ignore the very real possibility that he was avoiding me on purpose.

"I wouldn't be surprised." I tossed a bouncy ball against the slanted ceiling of her attic bedroom. We were lying flat on her bed, and I was hitting a poster of Grace Jones in the face with the ball again . . . and again . . . and again.

Kendall sat up and batted at the ball, sending it bouncing down the trapdoor into the hallway. I made a little whining noise as I listened to it retreating down the hall. "Stop it," said Kendall. "I'm sure he's just busy."

I made another little whining noise and rolled over onto my side. "I know. I was just hoping I could talk to him."

"What's wrong with me. You can't talk to me?"

I made a face at her, and she imitated it.

"Well," she said, "if he turns out to be a jerk, I will take full responsibility."

"Yeah? What are you gonna do to make up for it?"

"I'll make sure you never make the mistake of dating a buff football player with a heart of gold again, that's for sure."

"We're talking *if* he turns out to be a jerk."

"Right," said Kendall. "Which we both know isn't true, so it's fine. He's probably got family drama or something going on."

"Probably not. His family is, like, *perfect*."

"Why, have you met them?"

"I've seen their house. It was like something out of Martha Stewart."

"You do know Martha Stewart went to jail, right?"

"Martha Stewart went to jail? When?"

Kendall glared at me for a second, and I cracked up. Her response was to attempt to suffocate me with a pillow.

"So you still have that chip in your butt or what?" she asked, when I had finally tapped out.

"Yeah. Getting it removed tomorrow."

"You need me to come hold your hand?"

"I think I'll be okay."

"I never liked the idea of those chips in the first place. You know that."

"Yeah." I stared up at Grace Jones's judgey face. "What . . . do you think? About the Legion, I mean."

Kendall rolled away and lay next to me. "I don't know. You know I'm not a big fan of, like, corporations and big government and all that shiz."

"Commie."

She smacked me with the pillow again. "I mean, I don't know if they're really good or bad. I think they're just a big group of people, and most of them are trying to do the right thing, and you gotta decide if that's something you feel like you should be a part of."

"I don't feel like I should be a part of anything."

"I know. Well, I wouldn't complain if you threw in the towel, you know that. I don't like seeing you with all these bruises and stress."

"I can't do that."

"Yeah, I know." Kendall lifted her head to look at me. "So that answers your question, doesn't it?"

By the time two days passed, I was almost convinced that Rick had just decided to break up with me, and was avoiding me in order to get out of having to do it. Skipping school didn't really seem like his style though, and neither did avoiding me. I'll admit I got a bit worried about him, so after I got my butt chip out (just as fun as it sounds, believe me), I went over to his house and rang the doorbell.

A pretty middle-aged lady with a ponytail and yoga pants answered the door. To her credit, she didn't immediately look disgusted and tell me to get off her property. Instead she just seemed a bit confused and surprised. "Can I help you?"

"Um, I'm a . . . *friend* of Rick's." I swallowed hard when I realized that I actually had no idea whether Rick's parents knew he was gay. And, I mean, I didn't have like a full-on lisp, but I didn't exactly give off hetero vibes either, so if they didn't know, they were either going to assume that Rick just had a very diverse group of friends or else . . . I don't know, I was some weird gay kid who was stalking their athlete son.

I was overthinking the whole thing, of course, and Rick's mom just stood there looking politely at me. "Oh. Well, Rick's been under the weather. I don't think he's up for visitors. You could try texting him."

"Yeah. Uh. I'll do that." I hoisted my backpack onto my shoulders and trotted off as quickly as I could, my face going hot. I turned the corner and glanced up at Rick's window as I walked past it. The curtains were drawn.

That night I was at last rewarded with a text from Rick. *Why did you come to my house?*

I sat cross-legged on the ledge I'd been leaning against, looking out over a busy intersection. Patrol was really boring a lot of the time. *I was worried about u! Is something wrong?*

Rick's reply took a while. I plunked my head in my hands as I waited, the bright colorful lights of the city going blurry behind my unfocused eyes.

Finally my phone vibrated again. *I'm just dealing with some stuff.*
Okay. U know u can always talk to me right?
I don't know Javi. Maybe we aren't compatible.

My eyes stung under my mask, and I threw my legs down over the ledge, leaning forward to catch my breath. He wasn't . . . he wasn't breaking up with me, was he? *Why are u saying that? Did I do something wrong?*

He texted me a quick *No.* Then after a moment, *I think it's me. I don't know. I can't talk about it.*

But I want to help you.

You can't.

Please? I hated sounding like I was begging. But I hated the thought of losing him a little more. He didn't respond, even though I waited up long after I was in bed that night, and finally dozed off with my phone still in my outstretched hand, waiting for him to text me back.

Rick wasn't in school all week, and I didn't get any more texts from him. I was starting to get really annoyed at him. I mean, it was one thing to break up with me over text, and a whole 'nother to do it in such a vague, cop-out sort of way. I was mostly just worried about him though, I think.

On Saturday I spent the whole morning in the business sector, helping a group of volunteers and heroes clean up some of the damage the battle had done. Captain Liberty was there too, cleaning up a different kind of damage by talking a whole bunch with TV stations and reporters, apologizing for what had happened, explaining the situation and what was being done to rectify it. I guess the Legion couldn't really afford a drop in action-figure sales, especially with a Hound to watch out for.

The Raven wasn't helping with the cleanup (she said she'd done "enough cleaning back in Czechoslovakia to last a lifetime"), but she did bring me lunch, which was nice. We sat on an overturned piece of concrete and talked.

"Were you born in Czechoslovakia?" I asked, and she nodded through her ham sub.

"Yes. A very small town there. My family was very strict and religious, so when they found out about me and my brother's abilities, they called us *čarodějnice*. Witches. We had to go to religious school, where they tried to work it out of us with cleaning. I never clean now."

"You have a brother?"

"Yes. Twin brother."

"Where's he now?"

She shrugged. "Don't know. Dead, probably."

"Oh. I'm sorry." I looked away, wondering why she was suddenly sharing personal information with me. Maybe because she'd seen me without my mask, so she wanted to return the favor? I wondered what her life was like, outside of being a superhero. Did she have a husband? A wife? Children?

"It was a long time ago." She glanced at me. "You don't have any siblings, do you?"

"How did you know?"

"You are used to being the center of attention."

I snorted into my drink. "You wouldn't say that if you met me in real life."

"Oh really? Is this not real life for you?"

"That's a good question." I swallowed the rest of my sandwich and crumpled up the wrapper. "Sometimes I think it'd be easier if this was the real me." I fiddled with my straw, making scraping noises as I pulled it in and out of the lid. "What if I just became Blue Spark all the time? Maybe it'd make all my problems go away."

"Don't you have a family?"

I nodded. "Yeah. But I feel like this is pulling me away from them anyway."

"Well." The Raven stood and hopped off the piece of concrete, helping me down as well. "I don't often give personal advice, so cherish this. Family, and a life outside of the Legion, it's important. So, you do whatever you can to keep from losing them. Even if it goes against what Captain Liberty says you should do. Hmm?"

"Yeah. I feel like you're my mentor or something."

"Ha! Just as long as you don't feel like I'm your grandmother. Now, I'm going to make Paulo eat something. Otherwise he'll talk until he falls over, and won't that be politically embarrassing."

She left, and I went back to sweeping up broken glass. I guess I was pretty into it, because it took me like five minutes to realize there was someone watching me from around a corner. He was wearing a hoodie and sort of backlit from the glare off one of the glass buildings that had managed to avoid being shattered, so I didn't recognize him at first. He was just standing there, peering at me, until I finally stood up straight and shaded my eyes to see him properly.

The moment I recognized him, he disappeared, vanishing around the corner. I dropped the broom and raced after him, against all my better judgment. "Hey! You!" I yelled, hoping to get someone else's attention. This was stupid, and the last time I'd chased after him, bad things had happened, but I couldn't stand the thought of him getting away. And why the hell had he been following me?

"Stop!" I shouted, just as he ran into a dead end and turned to face me. For some reason he was wearing his uniform, with the hoodie over top of it, but I recognized his mask and face underneath.

"I want to talk to you." He drew a ragged breath. He was hunching a little, but it only served to make him look bigger and scarier as he took a few menacing steps toward me.

"Don't come near me," I shouted, pressing the button on my belt to call for backup. "Last time you almost killed me. And why did you take my mask off?"

He laughed, his voice hoarse and angry. "I almost killed *you*? You're the one who can't leave me the hell alone while I'm trying to go about my business."

"Why are you here?" I was standing my ground, but desperately wanting to run away from him and the panic that was rising in me as he walked closer. I hadn't been scared of him before. But that was before he'd almost choked me to death. Before he'd seen my face, and might recognize me and my family next time we were out together. The little pit of anger in the bottom of my stomach swelled.

"Stay away from me," I said again, trying to sound threatening.

"Blue?" Captain Liberty's voice came from behind me, and I turned, relieved to see him and the Raven rushing down the alleyway toward me. Captain Liberty pulled one of his electric batons off his back, and the Raven lifted her hands, glowing purple energy surrounding them.

"That's Jimmy Black." My voice wavered a little. Damn it, why was I so scared of him?

Captain Liberty took a step toward Jimmy, who, to my surprise, backed away a little, looking wary.

"What are you doing here?" asked Captain Liberty, his voice calm. "There are over twenty Legion members just around the corner. What are you hoping to accomplish?"

Jimmy shrugged. "You saying I should run away?"

"You're a known criminal," said the Raven. "You assisted the Organization in stealing private information. We should take you in to the Legion for questioning."

And then Jimmy did something really, really weird. He glanced at me, locking eyes with me for a minute. And then he held his wrists out toward Captain Liberty. "Yeah. Yeah, arrest me."

"That's fishy," I said. "He's probably got a bomb on him or something."

But Captain Liberty didn't listen to me. Instead he went, grabbed Jimmy, and put his hands behind his back and freaking *arrested* him. And Jimmy just let him. He was holding his head down, and his expression was hidden behind the hood, but his whole posture was slumped. Like as soon as Captain Liberty touched him, he'd just shut down.

"There's something going on!" I hissed at the Raven as Captain Liberty led him away to the Legion jet.

The Raven nodded. "Yes, I agree. But I don't think it's what you think it is." She glanced at me sideways. Jimmy started to struggle, thrashing around in Captain Liberty's arms. A bunch of other Legion members rushed forward to help him, and I watched as Jimmy's hood fell back and he screamed, all the reporters' cameras on him as he was forcefully led into the jet.

"I have seen this kind of reaction before," said the Raven. "He's fighting the brainwashing."

Jimmy Black was taken into the Legion headquarters and retained in one of their fancy holding cells. I hung around outside with the Raven while Chelsea and Captain Liberty went in to interrogate him. When they came out, they were both exhausted and disappointed.

"He's definitely brainwashed," said Chelsea. "But he refuses to believe it. He's irate. It looks like the brainwashing slipped for a little bit. I don't know how. Maybe your fight jarred him." She nodded at me. "But he wasn't able to beat it completely. It's back, and he's not letting me in."

Captain Liberty sighed and tilted his head back, rubbing the base of his neck. He looked really old suddenly, although it might have just been the lighting. The rest of the Legion headquarters were bright and airy and modern, but the holding cells had been built in the eighties by the Organization, and you could tell. "I don't like keeping someone who's potentially innocent here. But letting him go back to the Organization could only be worse."

"My recommendation is that we keep him here," said Chelsea. "Try to keep him comfortable, and hope that he eventually decides to let me remove the brainwashing. It's the best we can hope for. If it's all right." She glanced at Captain Liberty. "I'd like to head home now. My husband's out of town, and I had to pay a babysitter last minute."

Captain Liberty gave her a small but warm smile. "Of course, Chelsea. Thank you for your assistance."

She nodded and left.

"Well." He turned to me. "With your help, we may have saved that young man from doing something he may one day regret very much. So thank you."

"Don't mention it," I said. The truth was, I felt awful. It was one thing to fight bad guys who were actually bad. It was another to realize that the person you'd been taking out all your righteous anger on is actually probably some polo-shirt-wearing businessman with like five kids. How many of the other villains at the battle had been brainwashed too? The dark underground cells here reminded me of the creepy underground prison at the Organization building, and I remembered with a shudder that terrifying old lady rushing toward me, her face all stretched and inhuman. What kind of person was she, to do that kind of thing to other people?

But I guess she wasn't really a person at all. Not anymore.

At this point you're probably like, *Oh come* on, *when is he gonna figure it out already?* Jeez, stop being so excited to witness my suffering. You rude person. But yeah, I am not, actually, completely lacking in a brain, so I did eventually figure it out. Specifically when I got a call from Rick's mom on his cell phone the day after next, explaining that Rick had vanished without a trace, leaving all of his things at home, and I was the only other person she could think of who might have some idea where he was.

"I'm sorry," I said. "I haven't seen him for days. Since before I came to your house."

"Oh. Okay." She sounded awful. Like she was barely keeping it together, but still desperately trying to sound civil and polite. "Well, we're going to file a missing person's report unless we hear from him. So, please, if you get any contact from him . . ."

"I'll let you know. I promise."

I put my phone back into my backpack and leaned against my locker, biting the inside of my cheek and trying to think of what could possibly be wrong with Rick. I went through every different possible explanation I could think of, all of them ridiculous and unlikely. Drugs? But he was on the football team. Maybe he was still really depressed over the car crash and suicidal? But he'd told me everything else, why wouldn't he tell me about that? I'd assumed he was just mad at me about something, but if he'd disappeared from home too, didn't that mean something worse was wrong? Where could he possibly be?

The textbook I'd been holding slipped out of my fingers and smashed onto the floor. Kendall had just turned the corner coming out of her home economics class and she looked at me confusedly, bending down to pick up the textbook and waving it in my face. "You got a problem with chemistry all of a sudden?"

"No." I blinked, but I couldn't seem to get my eyes to focus. I felt like they must be wide open in some weird caricature-of-fear-type face. "Kendall. What if . . ." I trailed off, unable to say it.

"What if . . .?" she prompted. "What?"

I took my book from her and shoved it into my locker, slamming the door to keep it from falling out.

"Hey, don't you need that for class?" asked Kendall, and I shook my head, backing away.

"I'm not going to class. I have to go to the Legion."

"What? Why?"

"I just . . . I need to check something. Can you cover for me?"

"What the hell do you want me to say?"

But I was already gone, Kendall calling a frustrated, "Javier!" after me.

I was barely outside the school zone before I ducked into an alley and changed into my costume, as quick as I ever had. I didn't have time to worry about being seen, or anything at all except getting to the headquarters so that I could reassure myself that it wasn't true. It couldn't possibly be true.

Except it could, of course. It all made sense. The way Rick had had to run off to work at the same times I had. The angry way he'd talked about the Legion. The way he'd avoided me after Jimmy had taken my mask off and seen my face . . .

I skidded to a halt in front of the Legion headquarters and went in the hero's entrance, rushing to take the elevator up to Chelsea's office. I must have looked wild when she opened the door for me, because she took a step back and her eyes widened. "What's going on? Blue, are you all right?"

"Yes," I said. "No. I need to see Jimmy Black."

"Why?" She narrowed her eyes at me. "Blue, you're panicking. What are you thinking?"

"I think I might know him." I forced myself to take calming breaths. "I think I might . . . I think maybe, if I'm right, I can talk him into letting you take the brainwashing off him."

"He hasn't been cooperative," she said. "But all right, if you think so. I'd prefer if you were a bit more levelheaded beforehand."

"I have to know," I said. "I won't be able to calm down until I see him."

I couldn't think. I couldn't begin to form feelings of hope or despair, or anything, until I saw. Until I knew.

Chelsea led me down, and the elevator took a horribly long amount of time. "You think you know his alter ego? You know we're not supposed to act on any knowledge we have about alter egos."

"But this isn't a normal situation," I argued. "He's brainwashed. I think the person I know is the real him, and Jimmy Black is who he was brainwashed into. I mean—" I brought my hand up to my face. "I don't even know if it's him. I have to at least see him, so I know if I'm just going crazy."

Chelsea peered at me. "You care for this person a lot, don't you?"

"Yeah." I took a deep, shaky breath.

"Then the best thing you can do for both of you is to go into this calmly, all right?" Chelsea hooked her arm in mine reassuringly. "It'll be okay."

I gulped down another deep breath, this one slightly less shaky. "Okay," I said, although my stomach jumped as the elevator stopped and the curved metal doors slid open. "I'll be calm."

We went down the dark hallways, and Chelsea spoke to one of the guards. She waited outside while I went in, past the layers of metal, electrified walls, until I was standing in front of the bars. They were reinforced with the same crackling red energy that had thrown the Raven across the room back at the Organization headquarters. Past the bars, Jimmy Black was sitting on a small metal cot, bent over and staring at the ground. He lifted his head a little when I entered, and straightened his back ever so slightly, regarding me through the jet-black mask that he still wore.

"Oh," he said in a low, annoyed voice. "It's *you*."

"Yeah." My own voice was too soft and fragile for my liking. "It's me."

He rolled his neck and looked away. His entire attitude was dismissive. Like I wasn't worth his time or attention. I took a step forward, peered through the bars. I waited, hoping that he would acknowledge me in some way, but the minutes stretched on. "You weren't at school," I said finally, so quietly I could barely hear it myself.

He shifted and tilted his head toward me. "What the hell are you talking about?" The lighting was dim and harsh, and I could only make out the lines of the bottom of his face. His nose. His jaw. His mouth.

"Your mom called me. She's worried about you."

He stood, suddenly and with force, and stepped toward me. "What," he said again, "the *hell* are you talking about?"

I could see his face now. I recognized his mouth—I'd kissed it—and the shape of his body, and the deepness of his voice, and *goddamn*, I was going to cry. I bit my lip. "You saw me. I know you know who I am: you took my mask off."

"Yeah. So?"

"So I know who you are too. How could I not? Rick, it's me." I reached up and took my mask off, lowering it from my face tentatively. He watched me, his eyes dark. I tapped my watch, turning the contacts on so that my eyes went brown, and watched his face, desperately hoping for a spark of recognition. "Do you really not recognize me? Have they brainwashed you that much?"

Jimmy ground his teeth. "I told them I'm not *brainwashed*."

"But those things you did. The people you hurt. That wasn't *you*."

Jimmy grinned, a horribly evil smile that distorted his face. "Oh, that's what you'd like to believe, is it? That I didn't realize what I was doing? That I'm this good, perfect innocent who was just tricked into doing bad things? Well, sorry to disappoint you." He turned away, breaking the eye contact that had held me in thrall. I felt as if he'd been stabbing me with a dagger, and now that he walked away, I would fall to the floor, my guts spilling out. "But I knew exactly what I was doing."

I stared at him, clutching my mask to my stomach as if it were the only thing holding me upright. "But you're not like that. I know you. What about the Rick I met? Was he just an act?"

He turned back to me, his face tight and angry, but he spoke in a voice that I knew completely as Rick's. "You know what your problem is, Javier? You see things in black-and-white. You can't imagine that someone might have more than one side to their personality. That a person can do bad things and still be a good person, or vice versa. You know, that's what I can't stand about you."

"Shut up!" I snapped. "I'm not that stupid, and you know it."

He crossed his arms and tilted his head back and to the side. "Obviously I don't know anything about you either, 'Blue Spark.'"

"If you're not brainwashed," I said slowly, trying to stay calm like Chelsea had said, "then why not let them check you out, just to make sure?"

Jimmy laughed, a proper, evil guffaw. "Like I'd fall for that. I'm not letting them rummage around inside my head."

"Someone's already rummaged around inside your head!" I shouted. "It's that Hound, that awful old lady!"

His eyes went dark again. "I don't know what you're talking about. I don't know any old lady."

"You're lying," I said calmly. "I can tell. You know who I'm talking about."

I was leaning too close to the electric bars. I could feel it sizzling on my skin. Rick—or Jimmy, I didn't know anymore—turned away. "You're wasting your time. I'm not letting them get into my head. And they can torture me all they want, but I don't know anything. You might as well tell my mother I'm dead."

"I'm going to tell her that you're okay. That you're safe."

"Yeah, you go ahead and do that. You're obviously a brilliant liar."

I wanted to leave then, to storm off in a huff. But I couldn't. "Rick," I said again, softly this time. "Please, I don't want to fight you. I'm sorry I did. I just . . . I want things to be like they were."

He didn't say anything. He was facing away from me, his arms crossed.

"I wish things were simple," I said. "I wish that neither of us were the way we are." I straightened up. "But we are. And we can still make things work. Please, Rick. Just let them remove the brainwashing."

It was like he couldn't even hear me.

"Rick," I said again. "Please."

"My name's Jimmy Black." His voice was hoarse. "Rick died in that car crash. Leave me alone, Javier. For your own good."

I left without talking to Chelsea. I knew she'd probably want me to talk about my feelings, and explain everything, but I couldn't. There was really nowhere that I wanted to go, though—nowhere that would feel safe, or would make me feel better for just a second. Except I wanted to go back down into that basement and into that cell with Rick. I wanted to rip the mask off, and make him look at me and tell me to my face that the person I'd met, and kissed, and let hold me wasn't real. Because I didn't believe it.

After I changed into my street clothes, I went walking. I walked for hours, from one end of town to the other, without realizing where I was going. Eventually I ended up on the south side of town, at the electrical plant where I'd gotten my powers in the first place. I hadn't been back since, purposely taking other routes home from school. Ones where there were more people around so I didn't have to worry about being attacked by bullies from school. Even though I didn't have to worry about that now.

It was easy enough to find the spot on the fence where I'd climbed up to reach the wire that my shoes had swung from. I was still wearing the shoes, although they'd gotten pretty ratty in the last year. At least now I had a job and could afford to buy some new ones. I probably should. I scuffed my foot against the spot on the worn concrete where I'd fallen, and sat next to the fence, leaned my head back on it, and looked up at the sky.

I wasn't going to give up on Rick.

No matter what happened. I just wasn't. Not until I was absolutely sure there was no hope left for him. And maybe it was stupid, and it would be better for me to make a clean break. But I wanted to help him. I wanted to save him. Otherwise what kind of hero would I be?

When I pulled out my phone, it was full to the brim with worried texts from Kendall, and I realized that it was nearly four o'clock. I booked it home, rushed up the stairs, and burst into the house, relieved to find that neither of my parents were home. The answering machine was beeping, and I listened to and deleted the message from the school about my absence, and then went and flopped down on the bed.

Rick's parents were worried about him. I had to call them, let them know that he was okay. Or at least not dead.

I waited until I had my breath back and then dialed Rick's number. It rang once and then a man picked up. "Hello?"

"Hi," I said. "Mr. Rykov? This is, uh, Javier. Rick's friend. I'm calling to tell you that I talked to Rick today."

There was silence for a few seconds. Then the man said, "I see. Where is he?"

"I don't know," I lied. "But he wanted me to tell you that he's okay."

"Is there a reason he couldn't talk to us?"

"I don't know," I said again. "I just wanted to let you know that he's, you know, okay."

Another long silence. Then, "Javier, is it? If I find that you're somehow involved with what's happened to Rick, I guarantee you I will not be allowing him to see you ever again, and we will be pursuing legal action if necessary."

"Oh," I said, because I really didn't have anything to say to that. I mean, I guess the guy was pretty worried about Rick, but jeez. "Wow. Okay. Well, I'll let you know if I find out anything else." I hung up and took a deep breath, thinking that maybe Rick's home life wasn't quite as picturesque as I had imagined it. I wondered again if his parents even knew he was gay, and why I'd never asked him.

Then my dad got home, and it turned out that the school had called him at work too to let him know that I'd skipped, so that was just a fantastic cap to an already stellar day. At least he couldn't ground me, because that would mean me missing work, and I knew that they kind of relied on my income a little bit.

I made sure to go to school the next day though, although I spent most of my two classes with Kendall explaining everything to her, so I'm not sure how much I learned. And then after school I got a call from Captain Liberty asking me to come into the headquarters to discuss "something important" with him.

When I got there, my favorite person ever, the Wolfhound, was lounging all casually on one of Captain Liberty's couches, his legs spread so wide that no one else could fit on the couch with him. The Raven was there too, and a couple of other Senior Heroes. Captain Liberty was behind his desk, and he gestured me to sit when I arrived. The Raven discreetly patted the couch next to her.

"There's been a new development," he said, once I'd sat down. "The Organization has offered a prisoner exchange."

"What?" I had a weird feeling in my legs, like they were going numb. I swallowed. "How many prisoners do we have?"

"Just the one, currently," said Captain Liberty. "Jimmy Black."

Pins and needles erupted in my legs, but I tried to stay calm. "Who do they want to trade him for?"

"They've offered us Lady Firebolt," said Captain Liberty, "Do you remember her? She was captured by the Organization ten years ago, along with her seven-year-old son, and also Sala, a Kanaan who was captured by them the spring before last."

"Three people," said the Raven. "For one of theirs. Why do they want him so badly?"

"I'll admit I don't know," said Captain Liberty. "But I'm considering the offer very seriously, regardless of that."

I sat still. I didn't know what to say. Part of me wanted to jump up and yell, *You can't! You can't send him back to them, they'll brainwash him again, even worse, and I'll never get him back!* But I knew, I *knew* how selfish that was.

"I don't think you should do it," said the Wolfhound. "That boy down there must be worth a lot to them if they're willing to trade in prisoners. That means he's worth a lot to us too."

"But Firebolt," said Lady Deathquake, a note of pleading in her voice. "Her son."

"All I'm saying is it doesn't make political sense," said the Wolfhound. "Not that any of you'll listen to me."

Captain Liberty regarded him seriously. "We'll have to put it to a vote."

The Wolfhound threw his hands up. "A goddamn vote. You might as well not bother, we know what the outcome'll be. People don't know what's good for 'em."

The Raven scoffed. "Oh, you were all for the vote when it was for something *you* wanted."

"So what do we do," said Captain Liberty. "The only humane option I can see is to exchange Jimmy Black for the prisoners."

"But he's a prisoner too," I said quietly. "He's brainwashed."

"It's three lives for one." The Raven put a hand on my shoulder.

"We won't give up on him," said Captain Liberty. "I promise. And we *will* stop the Hound."

CHAPTER FIVE

I didn't go to the prisoner exchange. I mean, I guess I should have, but I just . . . I really didn't want to. I was afraid I'd do something stupid like try to stop them. And I didn't want to see the prisoners either. I didn't imagine they'd be in very good shape. Luckily Captain Liberty didn't ask me to come, so I spent the night with my parents instead, watching some old Western movies.

There was a sort of tension between us now, even when we were relaxing together, that I hated. They knew that something was going on with me, and that I didn't want to tell them. The thing was though, I did want to tell them. I wanted to tell them everything. But I didn't even know where to begin anymore. I'd lied to them so much, it felt like I'd dug myself down into a deep hole. Telling them the truth would mean confessing to all the lies I'd told them, and I didn't want to hurt them that way. So I just stayed quiet and leaned on my mom's shoulder while we watched the movie and ate popcorn.

Rick was in school the next day. Of course. Any lingering doubt, or hope, that I'd had was finally dispelled. I could see Jimmy Black in him, even more than I had before, in the way he moved, and the tight way he held his jaw. Part of me wanted to kiss him, and relieve all that tension in him. But part of me also wanted to punch him in the face, and hurt him for all the hurt he'd done to me.

Unfortunately, I didn't get to do either, because he ignored me all day.

"I could go over there and give him a piece of your mind," suggested Kendall as I stared at him across the lunchroom. He was sitting with his football friends, eating, and looking sort of vaguely down and lost. "He deserves it."

"He doesn't deserve it." I shook my head. "But I am gonna talk to him."

I waited until lunch was over, and intercepted him on the way to his locker. He met my eyes for a second, and then tried to swipe past me, but I moved to block him. I must have looked pretty angry, because one of his friends whistled, and they all sort of backed away, leaving us alone together.

"I just want to know if you're okay." I took a step closer so that we could talk privately.

"I'm fine." He tried to shove past me again. I stopped him, and he glared at me. "Why are you talking to me?"

I raised an eyebrow. "Why wouldn't I be talking to you? I said I want to know if you're okay."

Rick seemed annoyed. "Of course I'm okay. We broke up, it's not the end of the world."

My heart skipped a beat. "I . . . didn't realize we broke up."

For a moment, he looked lost. "Yeah, I'm pretty sure we did."

I caught the confusion in his face, and suddenly realized what was going on. "Rick, do you . . . do you remember anything that happened?"

"Sure. There was, uh . . ." He blinked a couple of times. "An accident, and you got mad at me, and we broke up. It's fine, it's over."

"That's not what happened."

"Look, I don't wanna do this." He put his full weight into barreling past me, nearly knocking me off my feet. "I gotta get to class. Leave me alone."

I didn't leave him alone, obviously. After school I caught him again, this time as he was getting into his SUV. I jumped into the passenger side and shut the door. He gave me an affronted look.

"We *need* to talk about this," I said. "What do you remember? What did the Organization do to you?"

"They didn't do anything to me." He was obviously hopelessly confused, and I really, really wanted to help him.

"Rick, you turned yourself in to the Legion. Do you remember that?" He was just staring at me, so I continued. "And then the Organization offered a trade so that the Legion would give you back.

And now all you remember is that there was an 'accident'? They did something to you!"

"Well, yeah." Rick waved his arms. "I was a prisoner. It wasn't exactly fun. Why would I want to remember it?"

"Because!" I was almost shouting now. "You turned yourself in! After you realized who I was! You were fighting it; you knew what you were doing was wrong."

Rick's jaw was in a tight line, and his eyes were wide and dark. "Shut up."

"You're not a bad person, Rick! I know it!"

"Shut up!" He looked like he was about to lunge at me, and for a minute, I was terrified that he was going to put his hands around my throat and choke me again. "Get out of my car."

I fumbled for the handle and all but fell out of the SUV, sprinting back toward the school with pinpricks in my eyes and blurry vision.

After that, there was really nothing I could do. Rick did his best to avoid me, and I didn't see hide nor hair of Jimmy Black, not for a couple of weeks. The Legion and the Organization seemed to have come to an uneasy truce. Or at least a stalemate. Chelsea was busy helping the released prisoners recuperate. Their return was being celebrated, but Captain Liberty said that it would probably be several months before they were ready to see anyone. I couldn't imagine how badly the Organization must have messed them up, and every time I thought about it, I got a sickness in the pit of my stomach, thinking about Rick.

I wished I could talk to him, find out the origin of his association with the Organization, so that maybe I could get to the root of it and help him that way. Had he had his abilities before they got to him? Or had they done something to him? Rick had never mentioned anything that might hint at the truth.

Except the car crash.

So that was how I found myself sneaking into the school office late one night, and using my admittedly less-than-stellar hacking skills to get onto one of the computers and search for all the students in the system named "Vanessa."

It hadn't been my first choice, obviously. First I'd looked through all the internet and newspaper records, to try to find any information about the car crash. I looked through Rick's Facebook, all his friends. No one named Vanessa, although there was a Josh. The account had been locked, due to the fact that the individual was now deceased. Creepy how Facebook did that.

I'd finally found a picture in Josh's photo archives. A blurry photo that looked like it was taken at a campsite. Josh, a jock with blond hair; Rick, looking cheerful and a bit skinnier; and a pretty girl with short red hair. Vanessa, maybe? The image of her wasn't tagged. The other two were though, so it almost made me think that everything about her had been deleted, including the news reports about the car crash. By the Organization, maybe?

So yeah, the only other source I had been able to think of was to look in the school's computer files—even though I couldn't be sure they hadn't been erased too—but it wasn't like I could have been able to get onto an office computer during the day. I'd asked the Raven to show me how to hack into and turn off a building's security like she had for the Organization building, and then I'd gone in by, um, breaking one of the door locks. Accidentally, of course.

Like I said, I was definitely not a fantastic hacker, but I was able to bypass the computer's login system pretty easy, and it wasn't as if the school records were kept super secure. I just found all the people in eleventh grade a year ago, and pulled up the 1,731,748,961 *Vanessa*s until I found one with a photo of a girl with short red hair.

Yeah, I probably could have made that sound a lot harder and cooler than it was. *I hacked into the school's top-secret database, and retrieved covert information with my super rad hacker skillz. Also I wore sunglasses. At night.*

Let's move on.

So then on Saturday, I went to Liberty Fields, which sounded like a funeral home to me, but whatever. It was a big redbrick building with a pristine park next to it, and little white-framed windows. It didn't look creepy, really, unless you knew the building's history. Which, unfortunately, I did. Pretty sure Liberty City's school board got a commendation for its history program. And for scarring its students, probably. Anyway, I went in through the glass doors (complete with fancy locking mechanisms that you needed to press a special button to open) and asked if I could see Vanessa Larsen. They seemed surprised, and asked how I knew her, so I explained that I was a friend from school.

"All right," said the nurse, and she led me down the hallway.

The place was like . . . completely unscary, but also totally uncomfortable to be in. You know how rest homes are. Except that most of the people here weren't super old. I hunched a little, and felt guilty for hoping that none of them talked to me.

"Now, Vanessa has to be pretty heavily sedated most of the time," the nurse explained. "So she may not recognize you, and she doesn't talk much. You'll have to keep up most of the conversation on your end."

"Okay." I was feeling more and more like this was going to be a dead end. Should I really be coming here and upsetting an obviously mentally unwell girl by asking her about a traumatizing event in her past? I decided that if she got upset at all, I would leave right away. Possibly through a window. Because that wouldn't be traumatizing at all.

The nurse led me into a fairly big room with white walls and uncomfortable-looking plastic chairs. It was empty except for one person, sitting slumped at a table by one of the windows. There was a puzzle on the table, but she was ignoring it to stare out the window. She was wearing a white hospital gown over gray sweatpants and slippers, and her hair was in the same short cut it had been in the picture of her, but kind of flat and lifeless.

"Let us know if you need anything," said the nurse, and she left.

I swallowed and took a deep breath, inhaling the sickly sweet hospital smell that permeated the place, and took a few steps toward Vanessa. She didn't move at all. I wondered if she even realized I was there. I sat at the table next to her. "Vanessa?"

For a moment, I thought she wasn't going to respond. Then she turned her head slowly and looked at me, unblinking, her eyes strangely glazed.

"H-hi," I said. "You don't know me. My name's Javier Medina. I'm a . . . I was a friend of Rick's. Rick Rykov, do you remember him?"

She blinked finally, without any expression on her face, and looked back out the window. Her head inclined ever so slightly.

"Okay," I said. "It's just that . . . he's gotten into some . . . some trouble lately. And I thought you might be able to help me figure out how to help him."

"You can't help him." Her voice was surprisingly sharp, although so quiet I almost didn't hear what she'd said.

"Why not?" I asked, and she made eye contact with me for a minute, her eyes widening. Then she shook her head and swallowed hard.

"I don't know." She brought a hand up to her face. "I'm confused. I need my meds."

"Wait, but—" The chair scraped as I moved closer to her. "Did something happen to you and Rick in that car crash?"

She shook her head again. "No. I remember things that didn't happen."

"What do you remember?"

She looked more alert suddenly, and wary. "Why do you want to know?"

"I'm . . ." I bit my lip. "Um . . . can I tell you a secret?" A little jolt went through me, and I wondered if I should be doing this.

Vanessa shrugged. "Okay."

I glanced around nervously and leaned forward. "I'm a superhero."

Her eyebrows shot up, and an almost nonexistent smile touched her lips.

"It's true," I continued. "I'll show you." I reached for my wrist, and turned my contacts off for a second, letting my eyes glow blue for her.

Her eyes seemed to light up a little in response. "Are you on a superhero mission?" she asked, with a little trace of humor in her voice. "You need my help?"

I nodded encouragingly. "Whatever happened to you in that car crash, I don't think you imagined it. Rick . . . I think the Organization did something to him. But I don't know how."

Her face was different now, her jaw held tight and her eyes sharp. She glanced around, her lips white and trembling before moving so that our faces were almost touching. "Javier, right? Listen. No one died in the car crash."

I stared at her, trying to figure out what that could mean. "But the newspapers. Your boyfriend, Josh."

"He was already dead." Her voice broke, and she moved away from me, covering her mouth with her hands. "They killed him. They took us, experimented on us. Then they . . . then they crashed the car. They put Rick and Josh back in, but Josh was already . . ." She stopped and stared at me, her eyes wide. "I don't know, I wasn't there, I didn't *see* it. I just *know.*"

"What did they do to you? To Rick and Josh?" I took her hand, hoping that she could tell I wanted to help her. She was upset, and I didn't want to pressure her into telling me anything, but I needed to know.

She swallowed and calmed again. I think the medication she was on was keeping her from being too emotional. Also I'd heard that people who'd gone through traumatizing things were usually really calm about it, so there was that. "Whatever they did to them, it killed him," she said. "Josh. Not Rick though . . . something else happened to him." She shook her head. "I don't know, I don't remember. But—" she swallowed and looked at me "—when they tried to do it to me, it didn't work. I . . . I stopped them. I—" her eyes went wide "—I killed them. I ran away." Her hand was shaking in mine, and she grabbed me and pulled me close. "Am I crazy?"

"I don't think so," I said. Actually everything she said made perfect sense. In a terrifying way.

"I don't know how it happened," she said. "I don't know what I did." She shook her head. "Do you . . . believe me?"

"Yeah. It all makes sense. Rick can't remember what happened before the crash. You were supposed to be camping, but he doesn't remember it. And the Legion says he's been brainwashed by the Organization. They must have experimented on him, and then brainwashed him into working for them."

"God." She screwed her eyes shut. "I'm probably imagining all of this. The medication they give me . . ."

"I should get you out of here. You're not insane."

"But I'm still sick." She shrugged. "I have PTSD. Nightmares. I *killed* people, remember?"

"In self-defense!" I argued. "Listen, let me take you to the Legion. There are people there who can help you. Besides, you don't know that you're safe here. What if the Organization comes back for you?"

"I . . ." Vanessa looked frightened again. Her lips trembled, and she glanced at the door. "I thought it was just my psychosis, but . . . if everything else is true . . ."

"What?"

She was still staring at the doorway, her eyes glazed again, and her lips white.

"Vanessa." I wanted to shake her. "What?"

"I don't think they ever left," she said.

I glanced at the doorway to see that the nurse was back and walking toward us. Except something was wrong with my vision all of a sudden: everything going dark and inky. I stood just as the woman reached me, and before my vision went completely, I saw that her eyes were pitch-black.

She grabbed the collar of my shirt before I could react, and jerked me forward, sinking her fist into my stomach and sending me backward into the wall. I choked, trying desperately to get my breath back. Vanessa screamed to my right. I still couldn't see anything, so I used my echolocation instead, and the static image of some blurry, winged *thing* bending over Vanessa forced itself into my brain. Welcome to Nightmare City.

I sucked a deep breath in and threw myself forward, slamming into the creature with all my might and sending us both flying. A horrible screech temporarily blocked my echolocation, and I scrambled along the wall to reach Vanessa, grabbed her around the waist, and jumped up onto the window ledge.

I smacked a hand onto the paned glass, sending a ripple of noise through the entire thing so that it shattered outward, and launched myself out with Vanessa under my arm. Her weight was more than I was used to handling, but I managed to keep us up. As we went, my vision returned, and the blackness went away like it had never been there. Glancing back, I could see the nurse hanging out the broken window, her eyes like big gaping pits of nothingness staring after us.

I landed us on a nearby rooftop, and Vanessa dropped to the cement next to me. "They'll come after me." She stood and wrapped her arms around herself as the wind whipped at her hospital gown.

"You'll be safe with the Legion." I desperately mashed the button on my watch to call for backup. "We just have to get you—"

The gravel crunched behind us, and I turned to see the nurse, still in her flowery scrubs but with big shadowy wings framing her body. Her eyes were black, and way too big for her face. And then, of course, my vision went dark again.

I tried to use my echolocation, but that horrendous ear-piercing screech was back, completely blocking it out. I screamed at Vanessa to run, and then turned to where the sound was coming from, in time to feel a sharp, overwhelming pain in my stomach. Something an awful lot like claws dragged across my face, and I felt my glasses shatter, and closed my eyes just in time.

Angry now, I brought my hands up, shooting waves of sound at the creature. All I could think was that I needed to get it away from me, to get it off . . . I needed to see. But if my attack had any effect, I didn't notice it. From the way she was slashing at me, it seemed like it had only made her angrier. Like a giant pissed-off bird.

Another claw punctured my stomach, this one going deep, and I gasped, pain flooding through me and making me light-headed. My knees buckled, my vision went red, and for a moment I was certain I was going to die with that horrible screaming in my ears.

Then the screaming was cut off, and the darkness seemed to get a bit lighter. The claw in my stomach came free with an awful scraping feeling, and the nurse, now looking more like a big, black bird than a human, fell away from me. Vanessa was there, her hands retreating as the bird fell, and she took a step back and stared at me with her eyes wide and terrified.

My ears rang, sounds coming slowly and echoing, and everything seemed a little blurry and weird. There was noise like a jet plane, and wind was blowing on my face. Then I felt someone behind me, and instinctively turned to defend myself, but I could barely move. I recognized his voice anyway, it was Captain Liberty.

"Javier, what happened?" He pressed a gloved hand to the wound on my stomach, and I looked down and realized that it was, like, pumping blood out. Ouch.

"I need a med kit!" he yelled, and I guess I passed out for a second, because when I came to, he had lifted my shirt up and was putting gauze and stuff on it. I'd forgotten he was a doctor.

I squinted and tilted my head a bit, trying to find Vanessa. I finally caught sight of her slippers and gray sweatpants next to me. She was just standing there, staring at the dead bird-thing.

"It's dead," she said finally, her voice hollow.

"It was trying to kill me," I gasped, and Captain Liberty shushed me.

"Who are you?" he asked Vanessa.

She looked up at him. "Vanessa Larsen. I don't know what I am."

"She's a Hound," said Chelsea.

Captain Liberty turned from where he'd been sitting by my bedside. "Excuse me?"

Chelsea looked slightly out of breath, as if she'd run all the way to the health wing from her office. "A Hound. I'm sure of it."

"B-but . . . she can't be, she's only eighteen," I slurred. "I saw her school records."

"How is this possible?" said Captain Liberty.

"It was recent," said Chelsea. "The change. Probably when the Organization attempted to brainwash her. She resisted the initial break. That's how Hounds are created, remember?"

"You said it was really rare." I was trying not to cough or let it show that I was in pain, or else they'd put me under again. I'd had some pretty serious damage done, but I was going to be okay. Probably in a couple of weeks thanks to my Kanaan DNA. It still hurt a *lot* though.

"It is," said Chelsea. "Very rare."

"Can we trust her?" asked Captain Liberty, and Chelsea gave him a *look*.

"She's still human. She's a young, mentally scarred girl. What we can do is help her."

Captain Liberty nodded, and stood. "I'll speak to her, then, if you think that would be appropriate. Will you be all right here, Blue?"

"I have to call my parents," I said.

Captain Liberty turned back to me. "Have you thought of what you're going to tell them?"

I shrugged painfully. "The truth?"

"I can give them a call, if you'd like," he said. "Tell them to come visit you here."

"Yeah." I nodded. "Okay."

So that was terrifying. My stomach managed to keep doing flip-flops despite the fact that I couldn't actually feel anything below my chest. I didn't know why I suddenly wanted to tell my parents. By all accounts, this was, like, the worst way to break the news to them. I guess I was just so tired of lying, and feeling my own mortality, and also they couldn't be too mad at me when I was like this, right?

Wrong.

My mom yelled at me for, like, half an hour. She seemed furious about everything: the fact that I'd gotten hurt, the fact that I was a superhero in the first place, and of course the fact that I hadn't told them the truth from the start. They wanted me to stop, and when I told them that wasn't an option, they got all dismissive with me, and told me they were going to talk to Captain Liberty and make him fire me or whatever.

"It's my decision," I said over and over again. "It's what I want to do."

"But you're hurt!" said my mom, distraught. "Look at you!"

"I'm fine." Well, that was a lie. I was actually in, like, a lot of pain, but I didn't want them to know that, obviously. "It's just a job hazard. I was *saving* someone."

"Well who is going to save you, Javier?" She said it in English, which was particularly upsetting, and I don't really know why. I guess it was her way of saying that she didn't understand. Of all the ways I'd imagined of how them finding out about this would go, I'd always figured they'd be sort of proud of me in some way. Not just disappointed and worried. And that hurt a lot.

Captain Liberty came by that night after my parents went home. I'd never spent the night at the Legion before. I knew they had some pretty nice apartments where some of the heroes lived, but the health wing was just like any other hospital, and I didn't like it. The nurse was going to give me something to help me sleep, but the captain wanted to talk to me first.

"I spoke to Vanessa," he said. "I thought you should know: she's very grateful to you."

"I'm grateful to her too. She saved me. How is she?"

"She's having a hard time." Captain Liberty sighed. "She has severe PTSD, which was probably exacerbated by her treatment at Liberty Fields. She doesn't know how to use her abilities as a Hound very well yet, and she's suffering from guilt over the things she's done to survive this far. But I think she'll be okay."

There was a commotion at the doorway, and the Raven stormed in, looking angry. "I just got back from Alaska. I leave and you get hurt? *Tsk.* Always getting into trouble."

"It's not my fault," I said weakly. "I didn't think I'd be attacked by some harpy thing."

"No one does," said Captain Liberty gently. "I spoke to your parents as well."

"You told your parents?" said the Raven. "How did they take it?"

"They're mad," I said dismissively. "I knew they would be."

"They're worried," said Captain Liberty. "You can't blame them."

"Just thought they'd be proud." I sank down. "I don't know."

"Well," said Captain Liberty, putting a hand on the bedspread next to me, "for what it's worth, *I'm* proud."

I swallowed, and looked away. All I could think was that I'd just provided him, and the Legion, with the best possible weapon against the Organization. So yeah, of course he was proud.

I wasn't in school for a week after that, and when I did come back, Rick at least seemed relieved to see me. He actually talked to me, walking across the parking lot from his SUV to where I was sitting at a picnic table with Kendall. "Thought maybe you were dead." He shoved his hands in his pockets. "I see that isn't the case."

"I'm pretty resilient." I took a bite of my sandwich.

"What happened?"

I scoffed. "It was the Organization, what do you think?"

"I'll be right back." Kendall scooted off.

Rick sat down heavily across from me. "What did you do to provoke them?"

"I stole one of their Hounds." I was being deliberately snarky, but I didn't know what else to do. I was mad at Rick, despite knowing that nothing was really his fault, and I wasn't sure what the best way to break the news about Vanessa was. I hoped I could somehow cause his brainwashing to fail again, but I really had no idea how to do that.

"Not the old lady." I swallowed my food and looked at him. "Vanessa."

"What the hell are you talking about?"

"She's a Hound. The Organization took you and her and Josh and experimented on you and brainwashed you. She resisted the brainwashing; that's how she became a Hound. Sound familiar at all?"

"No." Rick shook his head. "What kind of bull is the Legion feeding you?"

"Vanessa told me."

"Well then *she's* been freaking brainwashed! Listen, Javier, you better not have upset her."

"Upset her?"

"She's mentally ill. She needs to be kept at Liberty Fields."

"She's traumatized, and she needs to be with people who can help her, not drug her and monitor her so that they can use her one day." I took another bite of my sandwich. "Anyway, it's her decision. She wanted to come to the Legion."

"Sure she did." Rick's eyes were ice-cold. "If I find out you've hurt her..."

"I haven't done anything to her. I was too busy being almost stabbed to death." I took a deep breath and tried to calm down. "She's fine. If you want to see her, you should come to the Legion."

"Ha. Like I'm falling for that again."

I threw my sandwich down. "Rick, *please*. You know what I'm saying makes sense. You know the Organization experimented on you, don't you? How do you think you got your abilities?"

"So what if they did?"

"*So what*? So everything!"

"Well, I don't care."

"You just think you don't care."

"That's it." Rick stood. "I'm not going to talk to you if all you're going to do is go on and on about brainwashing. I thought we could be civil, but obviously not."

"Rick!" I shouted after him as he walked away, but I couldn't bring myself to get up and follow him, and not just because my stomach hurt whenever I got up and down. I was afraid he'd start saying hurtful things again. Part of me just wanted to give up on him, and leave him to the Organization, since he was so damn stubborn about it.

After all, what was the use of saving someone who didn't want to be saved?

"Hey." Kendall returned, jogging back up to the picnic table. A set of keys was jingling in her hands. "I borrowed a jeep. You wanna go to the lake?"

"Um. What?" I tore my eyes from Rick's retreating form and stared at her. "Right now?" I had class, of course, and my parents would be upset, and, and . . . "Yeah, kind of."

It was a beautiful day. We drove out to the lake with the top of the jeep down, and then hiked over to a secluded beach. My stomach hurt from the exertion, but not as much as I'd expected it to, and when I finally lay on the beach, it hardly hurt at all. The water was calm and sparkling in the sunlight, and I pulled my shirt off so that I could sparkle too.

"Think if you go swimming you'll get superpowers?" I asked Kendall, who was stripping to her sports bra and shorts too.

She snorted and sat down beside me. "I hope not. Let me look at your injury." I lifted my arm so she could examine my stomach. The skin was slightly shiny, with a small, blue-tinged scar, but otherwise it had healed fine.

"On the other hand," she said, "if it gave me abs like you, it might be worth it."

"Oh yeah." I shielded my eyes from the sun. "Totally worth it."

"So this Vanessa chick," said Kendall, settling onto the sand next to me. "Is she pretty?"

"Yeah," I said. "And straight."

"How do you know?"

"I don't, I guess. She could be bi, but I know she had a boyfriend."

"Yeah, look how well that turned out."

I swatted at her. "You're horrible!"

"I'm just saying. Men are weak."

"Oh my god, Kendall," I sputtered, laughing so hard my stomach ached, although that might have been my injury. "You're seriously awful!"

"Yeah, but you agree with me."

"I'm not swearing off men just yet," I said with a sigh.

Kendall glanced over at me. "Now, you guys have officially been broken up longer than you were together."

"Yeah."

"And you're still into him."

I rolled over, letting the sun warm my back, staring down at the most-likely-irradiated sand. "I'm angry. I really liked him. Even *you* really liked him." I grabbed a handful of sand and let it filter out between my clenched fingers. "The Organization took him away from me before I could ever have him."

"Yeah," said Kendall, "but he's not yours."

"I want him to be."

Kendall sighed and got up. "Come on, let's go swimming. See if I can get me some superpowers."

We swam for hours, and by the time we got back to the city, it was getting dark. I climbed the stairs up to my apartment slowly, and tried to get past my parents like nothing had happened. Of course they were both sitting in the living room waiting for me.

"Where were you?" My mom got up and stood between me and the hallway. "The school called and said you weren't in your afternoon classes."

"I went to the lake with Kendall."

She raised her eyebrows at me. "Am I supposed to believe that?"

"It's the truth. Why would I lie? I mean . . ." I flinched. "I know I've been, like, lying about a lot of stuff lately, but—"

"You can't just skip school, Javier. What about college?"

"It's fine. I can miss a day every now and then."

"Javier." My dad got up and came to stand next to my mom. "What were you doing? Was it dangerous?"

"No!" I said, almost yelling. "We just went to the lake. I was having a bad day, and this is just making it worse."

"You can't blame us for being suspicious," said my mom. "How can we know you're telling the truth?"

"Because I told you the truth!" I shouted. "What do you want from me?"

They just stared at me.

"You don't even know," I said. "There's nothing I can do, is there? You just hate me now."

"We don't hate you, Javier," said my father, exasperated.

"Whatever." I shoved past them, slamming my door all dramatically. Okay, I know I was being stupid, but *they* were being stupid. I smashed my fist against the door one more time for good measure, and felt bad when it shook the whole wall. I didn't want to *scare* them. And I knew they must be scared for me. But what did they want me to do?

I pulled my shirt off, staring at the glowing lines on my body. They didn't get it. I'd still been doing my best to avoid letting them see me as any different, keeping my contacts in and only wearing long sleeves around them. Even though they knew now, I still felt like I was hiding from them, avoiding their judgment because I knew they didn't approve. I hated it.

I flopped down on the bed and pulled out my phone. I wanted to text Rick more than anything. But I didn't even know what I'd say. He probably had his own problems with his family anyway.

My parents are being awful. I typed the text out and stared at it.

I hit Send on impulse and swore at myself under my breath. What the hell was I thinking?

But of course I lay there staring at the phone, my heart racing, waiting for an answer. I nearly jumped out of my skin when the phone vibrated.

Why, what are they doing?

My fingers flew over the buttons before I could stop myself. *They're acting like they can't trust me. Even though I told them the truth. They're just acting like they don't trust me as usual and denying everything AND treating me like an awful human being at the same time.*

I sent it and flopped my head down on the bed. Why was I doing this? Why not text Kendall, or anyone else at all?

My phone vibrated again. *My dad did the EXACT same thing when I came out to him.*

Really?

Yup. It was all "You're just confused, it's a phase, oh, that's my son Rick he's super straight" but also, like, he'd get mad when I went anywhere by myself, and he'd act like I had some sort of disease.

My heart clenched up. *U never told me about that.*

It's not important. I don't let my dad's opinion of me define me.

Ya, but. I don't know. I'm sorry I never asked. I meant 2.

Well, too late now, isn't it.

I guess so. I sniffed and put the phone down. He didn't text back.

When my mom called me for dinner, I got up and put on a thin T-shirt, and turned off my contacts. I went out to eat and watched as they deliberately avoided looking me in the eyes. I felt a sort of hollowness inside myself that I was worried would fill up with anger. Luckily it didn't, just simmered down to sadness and aching, until I was lying in bed reading Rick's texts over and over again, and wishing desperately that he'd text me again.

Kendall was right. I was hopeless.

I ran into Jimmy Black a few days later.

It was completely a coincidence too. I was on patrol, and I got a notification that a break-in was happening at a gun store down the street.

A gun store. I know, safe right?

Jimmy's a terrible thief by the way. He just freaking walks into places in broad daylight and takes whatever he wants. For someone who's supposed to be really valuable to the Organization, he sure doesn't act like it.

So when I got there, the place was, like, deserted. Oh, the civilians were there, but I guess they'd been allowed to leave, because they were all huddled across the street gawking.

"Is there anyone still in there?" I asked a guy wearing a leather vest and a camouflage hat. How did I know he worked there, you ask? Lucky guess.

"He took the manager to the back," said camo dude. "We keep the good stuff in there. He's a big, mean-looking guy."

"Who, the manager or the thief?"

I didn't wait for him to answer. I ran inside, snuck up next to the door to the back, and peeked through.

I recognized Jimmy and sucked a bunch of air through my teeth. He was holding a guy, who I assumed was the manager, with his left arm cranked behind his back at an angle that would only take a slight tug to break, and waiting while the man tried to open the safe with one shaking hand.

"You're sure the good stuff's in there?" Jimmy's voice was cruel and mocking. "You're not just jerking my chain." He tightened his grip a little, and the manager cried out. "Hurry up."

"He's obviously left-handed," I said loudly. "He'd probably be faster at it if you weren't breaking his good arm."

Jimmy hissed and threw the guy up against the metal safe, turning to face me. "Oh, it's Christmas."

"*Feliz Navidad.* What are you up to, Jimmy?"

"Nothing that warrants the Legion's interest, trust me." Jimmy grabbed the manager, who had been trying to dash away. "Open it." He glanced at me. "March your little ass out of here, Blue."

"Oh, so you're not robbing this place?"

"What's it look like? Piss off."

The manager finally finished entering the combination, and the door popped open. Jimmy dragged the manager in front of him like a human shield, and backed in. "I need all the nuclear and restricted equipment you've got," he growled to him. "I know you're not supposed to have it here anyway, so why don't I take it off your hands?"

I stepped into the room slowly, giving the safe a wide berth, but moving so that I could still see Jimmy inside. The manager handed him two briefcases and a bag, which he hoisted over his shoulder. Then he grabbed the manager again and moved forward, with the guy still in front of him. "Come near me and I break his arm. You know I will."

"The Organization'll do a lot worse with those weapons if I let you get away," I replied. "Won't they?"

The manager nodded, and Jimmy smacked him on the side of the head. "What, you wanna die?"

"I'll go to jail now anyway," said the manager in a defeated tone.

"Well, you should have thought of that before you started selling illegal weapons on the black market," said Jimmy snarkily, and he shoved the guy at me full force.

I *did* stop to catch him. Maybe I didn't spend as much time as I should have making sure he was all right, but, you know. Judgment call. I raced after Jimmy, hoping that being weighed down by weapons would make him slower. I tackled him just as we got outside, which was fantastic. Like using blunt force to knock over a telephone pole. My body is not made for such rough interactions.

As we hit the ground, I heard sirens, and like three police cars showed up, screeching to a halt in front of us. Jimmy growled and threw me off him, but I managed to snag the handle of the big black duffel bag as I went. It split open, sending an impressive array of what I assumed were very illegal weapons everywhere. Jimmy glanced at the police cars, snarled, and hurtled the duffel bag at my middle.

I bent double as it hit me, and nearly fell over. Instead, I tossed it aside and ran after him, jumping over the frozen traffic and denting a car hood. Damn, he was fast. He rounded a corner, and I screeched after him, barely catching him as he burst through a back door. I reached it, admittedly a little out of breath (maybe I should take up football), and went through, ending up in an empty hallway.

"Jimmy!" I yelled, a bit of desperation in my voice. If I could find him, if I could *subdue* him, then maybe I could get him back to the Legion. Then they could work on breaking the brainwashing. If they didn't just agree to trade him again.

There was a noise like something falling over, and muffled swearing from behind a door. I darted forward, opening the door to reveal Jimmy hiding in a broom closet.

He tried to barrel past me, but I was ready, using my sound waves to throw him back against the shelving. "What, you thought I wouldn't find you here?"

"Screw off, I left the guns."

"You're more valuable than guns."

Jimmy snorted angrily. "Oh, don't start. If you even think the word *brainwashing*, I swear I will stab myself."

"You're not getting away." I tapped my wrist to signal for backup and stepped closer to him, anticipating his movements. I hadn't been this close to him in a long time, not since before . . . and damn it if he didn't look good in that skintight black suit. I was being stupid, imagining that he was staring at me with anything besides loathing. If I kissed him, would it break the brainwashing?

A flash of red light burned into my retinas. While I wasn't paying attention, he'd whipped a laser pointer out of his belt and aimed it at the floor, spinning it around him in a circle. I lunged forward, but he was already gone, fallen through a brand-new hole in the floor.

I smashed into the shelving, fell heavily down through the hole, and rolled just in time to avoid the waterfall of cleaning supplies that tumbled after me. My roll was terminated by a sleek red sports car, and its alarm started blaring as I crashed into the door. I shook my head clear in time to see Rick disappearing around the corner of the parking garage.

I got up and ran after him with my hands clutched to my stomach. The garage opened onto the street. If Jimmy got up there, he'd probably be able to get away before I could catch him. Then my watch beeped, letting me know that backup had arrived, just as a shadow passed over the entrance to the garage.

I made it out onto the street just in time to see several things. The Legion jet had descended between the buildings and had parked on the street, and across from it were several shiny black vehicles. Jimmy was booking it toward a black jeep, and the ramp on the Legion jet was coming down to reveal Captain Liberty. I pointed toward Jimmy, and

Captain Liberty must have seen the desperation on my face, because he nodded as if he'd decided something, and then time went all funny.

I blinked, and we were on the ramp of the Legion jet. Me, Captain Liberty, and Jimmy Black, his hands in restraints and clipped to the wall of the jet.

"What the hell did you do?" Jimmy shouted.

"What *did* you do?" I asked Captain Liberty.

"Well, I do have superpowers, you know," said Captain Liberty. "It's dangerous to use them too often—"

"Paulo!"

We all turned as the door to one of the black cars opened and a man stepped out. He looked completely ordinary—just some white middle-aged guy in a suit—but something about him creeped me out, even from all the way across the gap. Maybe it was the way Captain Liberty bristled. The man took a few steps forward, so that he was standing in between the line of cars and the jet. I recognized him as Williams, the man on the television back at the Organization headquarters. A few Organization members followed him, and Captain Liberty signaled for several Legion members to move forward too.

Williams spread his hands. "You have something of ours."

"He's not yours," said Captain Liberty, and Jimmy growled.

"I'm afraid he is," said Williams. "Jimmy Black is one of our greatest assets, and if you take him from us again, I'm afraid we'll have no choice but to retaliate. Can your public image handle that, Captain?"

Captain Liberty gritted his teeth. "This is an eighteen-year-old boy. Who you have brainwashed. You've infringed upon his human rights."

"If he didn't want to be with us," said Williams, "he wouldn't be."

"Javier." Rick suddenly sounded lost and scared. I ran to him.

"Rick. It's okay, you're safe, you're with me."

"I . . ."

Williams took another step forward, his henchmen following him. The heroes in front of us tensed, ready to fight. "Why don't we let Jimmy decide? After all, he has the right to choose."

Captain Liberty looked at me. At Rick. "I can't risk another battle."

"No!" I yelled, and turned back to Rick. "Rick, please."

Rick met my eyes, and for a moment he seemed terrified. Then something caught his attention, and he turned. I followed his gaze and watched as the car door opened again, and a little old lady in a flowered dress and a tan windbreaker stepped out gingerly.

"Rick!" I tried to shake him. "Don't look at her!"

But Rick was staring, his eyes wide and his body limp.

"Rick!" called the old lady sweetly. "Come back, Rick. You belong with us."

"No!" I reached for Rick's shoulders and kissed him hard, desperately hoping to shock him out of it. He bit my lip, and the sudden pain made me jerk away from him.

"Get off," he snarled. "Let me go." He glared past me, up at Captain Liberty. "You hear me? Let me go! I don't want to go with you."

"Well," said Williams. He was standing near us now, only the line of heroes between us. "You heard him."

"No," I said. "Please, Captain, don't let them take him."

"I'm sorry, Blue."

"No!" I could feel myself getting all gross and snotty, my eyes blurring up and my nose doing that awful runny thing when you're crying suddenly. I tried to drag him off Rick as he undid the shackles, but I was as weak as a baby, my hands shaking. "You can't do this!"

Captain Liberty let Rick go and gave him a push downward. The old lady was hobbling forward and met him halfway, reaching up to smooth his hair out of his face and lead him to the car. He didn't even look back.

I sort of realized that Captain Liberty's arms were around me then, and tried to shove him away. We both fell to the ground. "Leave me alone, you bastard, what kind of goddamn Legion of Liberty are you?"

"Blue . . ."

"No, shut up." I pulled my mask off, pressing the heels of my hands into my eyes. "Leave me alone, I don't want this."

Captain Liberty tried to put his hand on my shoulder again, but I swatted him away. I heard him stand and turn toward the front of the jet. "Take us back to headquarters."

Eventually, I got up from the floor and sat down on one of the benches that lined the side of the jet. Captain Liberty came and sat beside me. At least he didn't say anything.

"I don't want to do this anymore," I said finally. "It's all shit."

Captain Liberty was silent for a while. I got the impression that he kept wanting to say stuff and then deciding against it. In the end, he just said, "If you want to go on leave for a little while, that is of course, your prerogative."

"Yeah." My voice was low and brimming with anger. "I think I do. Really, really long leave."

It was weird to go back to the Legion building after that. I don't know why. It just felt like, I don't know, time should have stopped or something. At least long enough for me to lie in the middle of the street crying for a couple of hours. That was all I wanted to do. Instead I had to go get examined by the doctors, and then by Chelsea. Luckily she told me that I didn't have to talk about it right away, but I'd have to come back in a few days and get a letter from her if I wanted to go on leave. At that point I didn't want to go on "leave" at all, I wanted to quit. Which just goes to show how upset I was, because the Legion was the best thing to ever happen to me, financially.

When I left Chelsea's office, I was surprised to see Vanessa standing there waiting for me. She was looking way better. There was definitely still something fragile about her, and her cheeks were sunken, but she'd hidden it convincingly underneath some stylish clothes and makeup.

"Ivana told me what happened," she said.

"Ivana?" The name sounded vaguely familiar.

"Oh. The Raven. She's, um, letting me stay with her." Vanessa shrugged. "I couldn't live here anymore."

"I don't blame you." I went and sat on one of the benches across from Chelsea's office. The Legion building was set up like a really tall skinny donut, around a courtyard with big trees in it, so all the hallways are like balconies, open to the courtyard on the inside.

It's kind of scary looking down from that height, but I did it anyway. Vanessa came and sat next to me.

"You almost got him back," she said softly.

"Yeah. But I didn't."

"Not your fault."

"I keep thinking . . ." I sighed, and tilted my head back. "Maybe if he cared about me more."

"It'd be romantic," she agreed, "if his love for you overcame everything."

"I guess it doesn't work that way." I sighed. "I should just give up. Try to move on."

"Why?"

I turned to look at her.

"I mean," she continued, "if there was even a chance that I could get Josh back . . ." She sniffed and rolled her eyes. "Not that you should take advice from me, considering the state of my mental health."

"How are you doing?" I felt guilty suddenly. "I should have come to see you or something."

"I didn't want to see anyone." She shook her head. "I'm . . . scared. I'm scared I'll hurt people. I want to do good with my abilities, but I don't think that's even possible. And I'm afraid of becoming something, you know . . . inhuman."

"I don't know if Hounds are necessarily bad," I said tentatively. "Maybe it's just the one working with the Organization who is."

"Ivana told me that a group of Hounds captured her brother when they were teenagers." Vanessa flinched. "She said they tortured him."

"Oh."

"I don't *want* to torture anyone. It's not like I don't have free will, but . . ." She leaned back against the railing. "You know, the Organization, they *chose* the three of us. It wasn't just random. They observed us, and waited until we were going out of town, and targeted us specifically." She was looking down at her hands now, white against her skirt. "What does that say about us, that we were, like, perfect villain material?"

"I don't know." The thought made me uneasy too, but I didn't want to admit it to her. "Probably says a lot more about the Organization than it does about you."

"Maybe. Honestly, Javier, I don't know about me, but Rick . . . he was always such a good guy. If you can do anything to get him away from them . . ." She took a deep, shuddery breath. "Just, it would be good to have my friend back."

"Yeah, well, I . . ." I reached for my bag. "I don't know what I'm going to do. I feel tired. I'm going to take a break."

"You should come by," she said as we stood. "Visit sometime. Ivana talks about you a lot."

"Yeah," I said. "Maybe in a while."

"Javier."

"Hi, Mama." I let my bag drop to the ground as I slouched out of my coat. "Hi, Papa."

They were both sitting on the couch, the news playing quietly in the background.

"What happened?" asked my mom as I shuffled into the living room and flopped down on the old chair, lowering my face into my hands.

"I don't know," I said softly. "I . . . I quit. That should make you guys happy."

They didn't seem happy. "Why?" asked my dad.

"Because I don't . . ." I shook my head. "I *don't know*. I don't know anything at all."

They were both silent. I stared down at the orange rug through my fingers.

"I mean . . ." The words flowed out in Spanish like they never could in English. "They're so . . . they're so broken. The Legion. They're supposed to be this perfect force for good, but all they do is argue with each other, and they can't even save one person. I just want them to save him for me. And they can't."

A big ugly sob burst up out of me, and I pressed my hands to my face. I'd been holding it together so well all afternoon, and now I just couldn't anymore. "I wanted to do something good." I wasn't even sure if they could understand me through my crying, or if

I was even speaking anything remotely resembling proper Spanish. "I wanted to be part of something good, but I don't even know what *good* is anymore. I just wanted to help people." I looked up at them, swallowing down a heavy lump in my throat. "Why can't I do that?"

"You can." My mom reached out to take my hand. "Javier, you can do whatever you want."

"I can't," I said. "I don't know how."

"Then," she said, "maybe you need to help yourself first."

"Javier," said my dad. He glanced at my mom nervously. "We're very sorry that we reacted the way we did about . . . all of this."

I twisted my mouth a little.

My dad looked to my mom again, and she nodded. "You went through something very scary," he continued. "And you wanted to do the right thing, and that's admirable. And I'm sorry that you felt scared—"

"Yes," she said, "and that you felt you couldn't talk to us, or tell us."

"It's not your fault!" I said. "It's not your fault I didn't feel like I could tell you. You know that, right?"

My mom shrugged. "Who else's fault would it be?"

"It's mine!" I said. "I don't know how to talk. I don't know how to tell people things. I never have. It's easier to be quiet."

"We should have known that," said my dad.

My mom nodded. "We should have been able to tell. You know you never cried as a baby. You had tears, but you never made any sound. Just this little, pathetic wailing sometimes."

I gave an ugly snort. "Thanks, Mama, nice to know you think I'm pathetic."

"I don't think you're pathetic," she said, as my dad chuckled. "Javier, *cariño*." She moved to sit next to me on the chair, curling her arms around me. "We love you. I'm sorry we treated you badly."

"I'm sorry I'm a bad kid." I sniffed.

"You are the best kid we could hope for," said my dad. "It's just that we can't help worrying about you."

"Yeah." I wiped my eyes. "I know."

"But you're done with it now, right?" said my mom. "I think it's good. Maybe things can go back to normal."

"Yeah." One of my contacts slipped a little as I wiped my eyes, and I hurriedly straightened it. "I guess so."

I didn't go to school for a few days. My parents called and made excuses for me, which was nice. Kendall came over after school the first day and sat on my bed while I told her the whole story.

"Did you see him at school?" I asked. "How did he look?"

"Yeah, he's at school. He looks fine. Javier." She tugged the blankets down from where I'd pulled them over my head. "Are you, like, in love with him, or what?"

I glared at her. "We dated for like a week."

"Yeah, and you're still not over him. What am I supposed to assume?"

"That I'm a moron." I pulled the blankets up over my head again.

"Well, I never doubted that. So what are you gonna do about it?"

I told her that I was going to try to get over him, but instead I texted him again that night. I know, I'm stupid. Even not considering everything else, I was supposed to be taking a break from Legion stuff, not fraternizing with the enemy. But I couldn't help it, okay?

How are you?

He texted back, which I honestly wasn't expecting. *Fine. How are you?*

Terrible, thanks for asking.

I'm sorry you didn't get everything you wanted.

I ground my teeth. *I don't want to talk about it.*

So then why did you text me?

I guess I just wanted 2 make sure u still remember me.

You keep bothering me. I started to reply, but then he texted me again. *You're hard to ignore.*

I'm taking a break. From the league.

You realized how full of shit they are?

Yeah I guess. I mean . . . you were right about things not being black and white.

So you're just going back to being Javier?

Yeah. For a while.

He didn't text back, so I went and brushed my teeth, throwing a sweater on before going into the hallway, just in case my parents were still up. I didn't feel like being stared at, or not looked at, or whatever stage they were at now.

When I got back, there was another text from Rick. *I'm actually getting more training.*

I stared at the words. I thought about a million replies, but there wasn't one that wasn't rude and judgmental. And why wouldn't they be? I mean, it's not like I could tell from the tone of a text, but he seemed proud. He was proud of getting training so he could keep doing completely awful things for a completely awful group of people. How could I love someone like that?

I didn't text him back.

PART THREE

CHAPTER SIX

"**R**ick Rykov." The erasable marker squeaked across the board as the teacher wrote Rick's name on it before returning to the bucket of names to pick his partner. She pulled out another slip and squinted at it. Just like the bloody Hunger Games. "Javier Medina."

"You've got to be kidding me," I said under my breath, and glanced over at Rick, who was squirming in his seat.

"Um," Rick said loudly as the teacher turned to write my name on the board next to his. "Are we allowed to switch partners?"

The entire classroom burst out laughing. I didn't know for sure whether it was because they all knew we'd dated, or if they were just laughing at Rick's ill fortune in being paired with *that weirdo Jay-ver*. I had a feeling it was the latter.

"No," said Mrs. Kane. "That would defeat the purpose of random pairings."

She went back to pulling names, and I put my head down on the desk in defeat. When she was finally finished, Rick had to take all the initiative and come sit in the desk by me, nudging it with his foot to get my attention, like I had some sort of communicable disease.

"Hey," he said, and for a second I thought he was going to apologize. Instead he continued with, "Listen, I kind of need a good mark in this class. I have a football scholarship to LCU, and they're actually pretty strict about grades."

I scowled up at him. "Isn't it kind of unfair for you to play football?"

"How so?" He raised an eyebrow.

"Whatever." I sank my head down into my arms again. "It's not like you haven't done worse things."

"Javier," he said, obviously trying very hard to be patient. "Can we please just be civil? We've had . . . disagreements—"

"Ha!"

"—but that doesn't mean we can't work together on this like mature adults."

"Ugh!" I swung my head back dramatically. "My life is a farce."

"Javier."

"Yeah, all right, whatever. I want to get good marks too, anyway. I'm going to have to start looking into scholarships now."

Well, since I was technically only on a break from the Legion, I could probably still count on them to pay for my schooling. But as of right now, I didn't have any plans to go back to work at the Legion, so I was going to have to try to find another way to pay for school. Unless I wanted to actually make pizzas for a living.

"What are you going to take in school?" Rick's voice was tight.

"I don't know yet. General studies, to start with. You?"

"Politics."

"That's the funniest thing I've ever heard."

Rick's mouth curved into a small smile. "Then why aren't you laughing?"

I gave him a deadpan look. "I'm laughing on the inside." I rolled my eyes. "So what is this project even on?"

It was on the history of Liberty City, which was great because I grew up here and basically already knew literally everything there was to know about Liberty City, and awful because like eighty-five percent of Liberty City history was superhero mania disguised as actual history. Which, for those of you not following along rapturously, was exactly what I was trying to avoid.

I agreed to meet Rick in the library after school, and then bolted as soon as class was over to whine at Kendall.

"Seriously?" she hissed as I slammed my locker shut. "Can't you complain on the grounds of being morally against douchebaggery?"

"Um. That would probably infringe on his rights."

"Good. He infringes on our right to not look at pasty-ass muscleheads."

"Kendall. I appreciate what you're trying to do."

"I appreciate that you appreciate."

"It's okay."

She looked at me levelly. "Is it? Because I feel like this break has been good for you. From Rick and from the Legion."

I wasn't sure if that was true. Sure I had more free time, and my family was happy that I wasn't going out and putting myself in danger all the time. But the end of the school year was coming up, and stress about superhero stuff had been replaced with stress about school and graduation and university. I wasn't getting paid from the Legion now, and I'd had to spend a pretty decent chunk of my savings on stupid graduation fees, and my parents had had to cut back on our budget, which was even more stressful. I was even skipping prom because the last thing I needed to spend money on was a tux to stand around feeling and looking miserable in.

"I just . . ." I bit my lip. "I wish the Legion was better."

"Well, what do you want them to be?"

"I don't know. Just something I can feel good about belonging to."

"What's that gotta do with Rick?"

"Nothing I guess."

But it had a lot to do with him. Because Rick was *proud* of belonging to the Organization. And I guess I was jealous of him for that.

I brought it up the next day, when we were studying in the library. I shouldn't have, and I knew that, but I was getting tired of acting like there wasn't a huge elephant just, like, chilling out behind us the whole time. We were taking notes about the Organization, and I said, sort of offhand, "I don't know why anyone would want to be part of a group of villains."

Rick rolled his eyes. "Because I feel like I'm doing something. You know, something that will make a positive change. You're automatically associating the word villain with something bad."

I hunched over my notes "I thought we weren't gonna talk about it."

"You're the one who brought it up!"

"Yeah, but like. In a theoretical way."

Rick leaned forward, lowering his voice. "I'm just saying, you have to admit the Organization made some pretty radical changes when they were in power. And some of them are still in effect because they were *good* changes."

I glanced up at him, annoyed. "So?"

"So." Rick scrunched his nose up in a way that was far too attractive considering the crap that was spewing out of his mouth. "Sometimes you have to do things that might seem bad, or even evil, but for the purpose of the greater good."

"Okay Rick—" I shoved my book away and turned to face him. "Do you wanna know who you sound like?"

Rick leaned back in his chair and crossed his arms. "Sure. Who?"

"Hitler. You sound like Hitler."

Rick's face broke into a grin that was completely devoid of cheer. "You're really gonna compare me to Hitler. You're gonna go there."

"Oh, I went there."

"You're a child."

"How is that childlike? You have similar political policies!"

"You have similar political policies to a piece of sh—"

"*Shhhhh!*" the librarian hissed across the library at us, so loudly that my ears actually hurt a little. She finished her assault on my eardrums and sat there, giving us the most horrific stinkeye I'd ever seen in my life.

"Right." I gathered up my books, my face hot. "I'm leaving."

"Good. We'll finish this later."

"Fine."

Rick waved me away, and went back to his book. "Fine."

"You shouldn't have compared him to Hitler," said Ivana firmly. "Mussolini would have been more accurate."

Vanessa snorted and set a bowl of popcorn down on the table. "It's so . . . not like him to say something like that."

"Well," I sighed. "He's brainwashed, right? But it really did seem like he believed it."

"You have to get to the root." Ivana took a handful of popcorn while counting her Monopoly money with one hand. "This is the way Hounds work. They find the fragile parts of your mind and make you believe something you never thought before. They can change anything."

"But it can be reversed, right?" I glanced at Vanessa.

"Yeah, if they're willing. Which, I guess, they aren't usually."

"For obvious reasons," said Ivana. "How would you like if you found out that something you thought you believed was put in your head by someone else?"

Vanessa and I shuddered in unison, and Ivana *tsk*ed. "If that boy is all you two are going to talk about while you are here, Javier, I will make a ban on the subject."

"I'm honestly trying to get over him." I slouched in my chair. "I mean, he's obviously either a fascist, or happily brainwashed. Or both. And I don't want to be with a guy who's either."

"That's good," said Vanessa. "Standards are important. I have three hotels on that square, by the way."

I sighed, and handed over what felt like all of my money. "So is it okay if I interview you for my project?" I asked Ivana. "It's about the Legion."

"Hmph. Depends what kind of light you are going to put the Legion in," she said testily. "You have some sort of grudge against us right now, don't you?"

"Not a grudge." I shrugged. "I just feel like . . . they could do better."

"Better like the Organization?" asked Vanessa.

"No!"

"Well." Ivana rolled the dice, and picked up a card, frowning at it. "Ethics are pesky things, aren't they? Why don't you interview Captain Liberty?"

I was shocked when Captain Liberty actually agreed to meet with me for an interview. As if he didn't have better things to do. I didn't even know why I was doing it, except that it would probably guarantee me a better mark, and that was the least he could do for me. Besides that, some small part of me did want to put the Legion in a positive light, if for no other reason than to have some ammunition to use against Rick when he made little snide comments about the Legion.

"They don't do anything," Rick had said during a particularly heated argument that we'd had to take out to the picnic tables beside the library. "They're just a way to make profit off people who actually want to do good."

"So what, heroes don't deserve to get paid for what they do?"

"That's what the police are for! And anyway, crime still happens, whether or not you have people out in spandex fighting it." Rick crossed his arms. "You have to treat the source, not the symptom."

"Right, by taking over the world and forcing everyone to do what you want."

"How is that different from the Legion?"

"Because it is!" I shouted. "Because the Legion doesn't torture people, or brainwash them. At least they're trying to do good."

"Doesn't mean they are, though," said Rick. "You shouldn't just blindly support them."

It kind of threw me for a loop when Captain Liberty had pretty much the exact same advice for me when I met him in his office for our interview.

"I encourage everyone to question the Legion." He steepled his hands. "Unfortunately, lack of productivity is the price of encouraged dissent. The fact that you are not currently working for us, for example."

I finished writing down *lack of productivity is the price of encouraged dissent* and looked up at him. "Did you ever want to quit?"

"I did," he said softly. "I had thoughts that I could do better on my own, that the Legion was broken, that it had never worked. But . . ." He shifted in his seat. "There's some part of me that strongly believes in the power of intent. A group of people truly dedicated to making the world a better place, even if a lot of the time we fall short of our goal, or we . . . make mistakes that hurt people." He glanced at me. "That's a group of people I want to belong to. I'm afraid I can't speak for anyone else."

I think he meant it as an apology for not being able to save Rick. And I felt bad suddenly, like really crappy, because it was obvious that he had tried really hard. He looked tired, sitting behind that desk, with that heavy cape hanging next to him, and I wondered how many people he'd tried and failed to save. How much weight was on his shoulders?

"What's your superpowers again?" I asked. "I know it's something about time."

"I can manipulate time, yes." He looked grateful for the change of subject. "Slow it down, freeze it. Even go back and change things."

"How often do you do that?" I swallowed uneasily. How many times had he redone a conversation with me? How many times had that moment with Rick on the jet happened?

"Never," he said, and I deflated with relief. "I occasionally freeze time, but even that can be dangerous. When I was young, I manipulated time on a whim, changed things constantly. Until I realized that every time I changed something, I created an entirely new universe, and unfortunately, I don't have the ability to maintain universes. They all collapsed. Except this one, of course. I had to go back to the very beginning, to stop it all from happening."

"Were any of those universes better than this one?"

He smiled at me sadly. "Of course. Every one." He paused, and then cleared his throat, reaching forward to straighten some papers on his desk. "Is this good? For your paper? Or do you need more history? I can tell you almost anything you want to know, going all the way back to the sixties, if my memory holds."

When I got home that night, I changed into a tank top, took my contacts out, and climbed up onto the roof. It was a bad idea to be going around with my markings showing and my eyes all glow-y, but it was *so* hard constantly having to cover myself up and hide how I really looked. I just needed a break. A chance to be myself.

And I had a lot of thinking to do.

It was both selfish and immature of me to expect the Legion to be the perfectly good entity that the media tried to make it out to be. When I'd joined, I'd thought that the Legion members were the good guys, and the Organization were the bad guys. But I knew now that there were no good guys, just people trying, and sometimes failing, to do the right thing. Maybe there were no bad guys either.

Except no, I knew there were. The people who experimented on Rick and probably countless others, who killed and hurt people when they were inconvenient, they weren't good. And they weren't trying to be, no matter what Rick thought.

I had abilities, gifts, whatever they were, and I knew deep down that I couldn't ignore them forever. It was who I was, as much as the glowing blue marks on my skin and my attraction to muscly guys were. I had to choose, whether to use my abilities for personal gain, for power, or to try my best to do good, to do the right thing, even if I didn't always *get* it right.

And that was what the Legion was. Not a perfect force for good straight out of a comic book. Just a group of people trying to do the right thing. And that was why I belonged with them.

"Javier?"

I turned to see both my parents scrambling their way up over the fire escape onto the roof, their bathrobes wrapped tightly around them.

"Careful." I knew that in the dark shadow of the water tower, with only my glowing eyes and markings visible, I must look more than a little inhuman. "I'm not wearing like five layers and glasses. You might see something you don't want to see."

They picked their way across the roof toward me, and I kept eye contact with my mom until they were both standing right in front of me.

"Hi," I said. "I'm sorry, I needed to think."

"It's not safe up here," said my mom with a tight gesture.

"So go back down."

"Is something wrong, Javier?" asked my dad, and I laughed.

I was sitting on the little platform under the water tower, and my mom came and sat down next to me, my dad following. I inched away and bunched my shoulders reflexively, suddenly feeling self-conscious. My mom reached forward and touched my face, bringing my chin up so that she could meet my eyes. I don't know how I must have looked. Scared, I guess, and a bit angry. I just wanted her to see me and accept me. I wanted to tell her that, but at the time, I couldn't think of the words.

She hesitated for a few seconds, then smoothed my hair out of my face. She touched the markings on my arms, tracing them with her finger.

"Do they hurt?" she asked, and I shook my head.

"Not now."

"But they're the reason you keep getting hurt."

"No!" I said. "Well, maybe, indirectly, but it's mostly my fault for not thinking things through and for fighting people bigger than me. Mama, the point is . . ." I grabbed her hand, and made her look up at me again. "Do you know how many people's lives I've saved in the last year?"

"We don't care about people we haven't met, Javier," said my father. "We care about you."

"It's eighteen," I said. "And those are just the people that I *know* for sure would have died if I hadn't been there. Eighteen people. Maybe that doesn't seem like a lot to you, but it does to me."

"But what if *you* die, Javier?" My mom's hand was tight on mine, and her voice was shaking. "What will we do then?"

I felt like my heart was breaking. "I'm sorry. But I have to. I just have to, please understand. It's who I am."

"It's not fair," said my father. "We should have had a son who was a coward."

"I'm sorry," I said again, my breath catching as I drew it. "I'm sorry that I'm not the way you want me to be, I'm sorry that I can't change back—"

"Shush." My mom brought a finger up to my mouth. "Don't ever be sorry for that, *cariño*. You know, this is just something your father and I have to deal with."

My dad nodded. "She's right. And we're sorry that it's taken time, and that we hurt you in the process."

"It's okay," I said. "I mean, I've had a lot going on. I just . . ." I sucked in a deep breath, glancing away at the horizon, and then back at my mom. "I want to . . . be able to be myself with you guys. I know it's not easy, but I want us to be honest with each other. And," I said as they nodded, "I want to go back to the Legion. I want to keep trying."

I had only been back to work as Blue Spark for a couple of weeks before I ran into Jimmy Black again. Official nemeses, us. Okay, so I'll admit, this time it wasn't entirely a coincidence. Rick and I had met up at the public library to do some more research for our project, and he'd gotten a suspicious call and had to leave. It was a good thing, anyway, since we'd just been arguing again. Apparently Rick had gone and interviewed an Organization member, since I'd interviewed Captain Liberty. The guy he'd talked to was Black Orb, a retired villain who was a big deal in the seventies.

"He's super mellow now," Rick had told me matter-of-factly. "He lives at the Organization headquarters, and he gets a pension. I, uh . . . I asked him about the Hounds."

"Really?" I was curious despite myself. "What did he say?"

"Uh." Rick rolled his eyes. "That if I even know about them, they must not have as good of a hold on me as they think they do."

"Seriously?" My heart started to beat fast, and I stared at Rick. "So he admitted they've done something to you?"

"Yeah, according to him. But, listen Javier, I don't really care that much."

"Of course you don't! They've made you not care."

"Maybe." Rick shrugged. "Why's it matter anyway?"

I had seriously never been more frustrated with a human being than I was with Rick in that moment. And it wasn't even his fault. But I didn't care.

"Rick—" I said loudly, too loudly for the library, and then of course, his phone rang.

He gave me an annoyed look and answered. "Yeah," he said quietly. "Yeah, I can do that. I was just finishing up anyway." He shoved his phone into his bag. "Gotta go."

So yeah, I followed him. And there was a shiny black car waiting empty outside the library for him, and he got into it and drove off. Seriously, the Organization let Jimmy Black use one of their cars, and the Legion wouldn't even give me a waterproof suit.

It was rush hour, and traffic was pretty bad, so I managed to keep track of the car, following along the rooftops until it stopped at an old row house. I watched from a rooftop opposite while Jimmy Black got out and went up to the front door. He knocked and waited, hands on his hips, until the door cracked open. Then he kicked it in and grabbed the guy who had opened it by the scruff of his neck, dragging him down the steps and shoving him into the back of the car. Or at least, tried to. I jumped off the roof and sprinted toward him, stopping him just in time.

"Are you serious?" growled Jimmy as the guy took off running down the sidewalk. He tried to go after him, but I stood in his way, aiming a shock-wave-reinforced kick at his kneecap that sent him rolling to the ground. "Don't make me pummel you, Javier."

"It's Blue."

"You followed me from the library. That's against code, so I'll call you what I want."

"What were you going to do with that guy?" I asked as the man disappeared around the corner. Jimmy made an annoyed noise.

"If you have to know, I was gonna take him to a bank and make him take out money. He's owed the Organization for like ten months now."

"Really." I crossed my arms. "That's it."

"Don't believe me if you don't want to, but yes." Jimmy took a step toward the car.

I stopped him. "We need to talk. We really, really need to talk."

"Why?"

"Because." I sighed. "I need to get over you."

He gave a forced laugh. "You're not over me by now?"

That hurt. I ground my teeth. "Look, can we just go somewhere private and talk?"

"Yeah right. You'll take me to the Legion."

"We can go in your car."

"How do you know I won't take you to the Organization?"

"After the Legion voluntarily gave you up instead of capturing you again, the Organization kidnapping me would be a really, really bad move."

"Sure," said Rick. "If you think so." He walked around to the driver's seat and got in. "We'll talk in the car."

"Not in the car," I said. "It could be bugged. Take me up to the point."

This was it, I told myself. My last-ditch effort to get Rick to listen to me. To get him back. We drove up to a secluded spot a bit past the point, and got out to go sit on a bench, watching the sun set over the city.

"Okay," said Rick. "I don't see what you have to discuss with me that you couldn't before, but let's hear it."

"I need you to be honest with me. Can you do that? Promise?"

"I have nothing to hide."

"Do you still like me?"

The question seemed to take him by surprise. "Like *that*?" He paused. "Yeah, I do. But I don't see how it could possibly work, since I see you're back with the Legion now, which kind of makes us enemies in every way."

"Why did you choose them over me?" I hated how pathetic and needy that sounded. "Why is it so important that you belong to that group, one that you know has hurt people and done terrible things?"

"Honestly? Because I did say I would be honest." Rick leaned back on the bench. "I just feel . . . right with them. I feel at home. They're like family, you know? You can't betray your family. You just can't."

"But what about your *real* family?"

"What about them?"

"It's just, the Raven told me that the Hounds work by getting into people's heads and latching on to the places where they're fragile, so I thought—"

"Javier, honestly. Stop trying to psychoanalyze me. That's the last time I'm going to ask." Rick looked at me seriously, his eyes a deep and rich brown in the setting sun, even with the shadow of the mask over them. "I need you to *get over me*. Can you do that?"

"Why?"

"Because." Rick waved his arm. "I can't have these weird doubts and suspicions in my brain. I need to be able to focus on the Organization, and not think these kind of . . ." he gestured again, frustrated, "thoughts. I need you to give up on me, so that I can give up too."

"Give up on what?"

"I don't know." He slumped. "Everything."

"Oh god, Rick." My voice broke. There were a million things I wanted to say, a million arguments that I knew he wouldn't hear. "Please, please don't."

"Don't tell me what to do," he said angrily.

"I'm not!" I leaned forward. "I'm *asking*. I'm begging you. I'm just . . ." I brought my hands up, clenching my fingers, wanting to grab him and never let him go. "I don't want to lose you. I'm terrified that one day I'll see you and they'll have taken all of you away, and you won't even recognize me anymore. I don't want that to happen, because I—"

"Don't." Rick stood up. The sun had set anyway, and there really wasn't much more to see. "I'll drive you back to town. Just leave me alone, Javier. There's no hope for me."

Two nights later I got a call from an unknown number at three in the morning. I flailed around in bed and knocked my phone onto the floor trying to grab it, and ended up answering it while hanging upside down from my bed.

"Hullo?"

"Javier. It's Rick. I don't have much time, I'm calling you from a pay phone."

I sat up, kicking to disentangle myself from the blankets. "What's wrong?"

"I'm on a mission with the Organization. We've been sent to kidnap a lady, and bring her back for processing."

"Processing? What's that mean?"

"Nothing good." Rick was breathing heavily. "Javier, listen, I—I need you to stop me."

I froze in the midst of getting out of bed. "What?"

"I can't do it myself. If the Organization realizes I've disobeyed them, they'll—"

"They'll give you to the Hound again," I finished for him. He knew. He knew and he was asking me to help him. I wanted to dance for joy, but all I could feel was dread and fear.

Rick sounded rushed and desperate. "I don't want that to happen. Please, Javier, you have to stop me."

I got out of bed, fumbling around for my costume. "But won't they punish you?"

"I'd rather be punished than brainwashed again."

"I understand." I finished pulling on my costume and hopped up onto the windowsill. "Where are you?"

It didn't quite feel real, being out so late at night. I guessed that once I stopped being a Junior Hero I'd probably have a lot more late-night shifts, but right now it didn't feel right. The city was too quiet, too peaceful, and I couldn't move fast enough through it. What if it was too late? Would Rick go through with it? Or would he disobey, and be taken and brainwashed again? What if afterward he didn't recognize me at all?

I couldn't stand that thought, so I focused on moving as quickly along the rooftops as I could, finally arriving in a back alley behind a pizza place where Rick had said he was going to be.

I crawled along a fire escape and crouched in a shadow, waiting as fear tickled my stomach like ants. I wished I'd had time to call Captain Liberty, but there was only so much he could do anyway. For the Legion to interfere in this again would probably start a war. Rick wasn't worth a war, but damn it, he was for me.

A car door swung open below me and four figures emerged from it. I recognized Jimmy Black's bulky figure, and then two slightly smaller guys. In between them they were holding a petite woman with what looked like a cloth bag over her head. She was struggling as they dragged her down the alleyway, and one of the Organization guys kneed her in the stomach and turned to Jimmy. "What the hell are we doing here?"

"Switching vehicles," said Jimmy hoarsely. "No surveillance footage here, so the transfer will be untraceable."

"All right, smart guy," said the crony, grunting as the struggling woman attempted to knee him in the crotch. "But how come we gotta deal with the b—"

I dropped on him from above, wrapping my knees around his head and grabbing the fire escape above me to twist him to the ground. I pulled myself up out of the way just in time as the second guy ran at me, and he slammed into the wall. He turned and raced at me again, running into my feet, and I kicked him hard in the side of the head for good measure.

In the moments it took for the two of them to get oriented, I dropped to the ground and broke the restraints around the woman's wrists. She quickly reached up to pull the bag off her head, revealing staticky black hair and wide dark eyes that looked relieved to see me. Then her eyes widened even more and she dodged around me to aim two sharp jabs into the eyes of one of the Organization guys, and then a kick to his crotch.

"Agghh!" yelled the guy. "Jimmy, get 'em!"

Jimmy gave an apologetic expression, and then rushed me. I let him slam me into the wall, not as hard as he could have, and his lips rested next to my ear for a moment. "You'd better hit me hard," he whispered, and when he backed up, his eyes were desperate and afraid.

I wanted really badly to kiss him, but instead I nodded and aimed a kick at his gut, sending him to the ground. I hit him with an uppercut to finish it off, and then took the woman's hand and tried to run with her.

I felt her tugged away from me, and turned to see one of the Organization guys grabbing her leg. She let go of me in a second and flew toward him, using his momentum against him to jam her knee into his stomach. Then she shot a clawed hand toward his neck, and pulled him to the ground. He fell, wheezing, to one knee, and then she took my hand again and we tore down the alley together.

I ended up grabbing her and flying several blocks south with her. Well, not really flying, obviously. I'm sure when most superheroes pick up girls and fly them around, it's all smooth and romantic. But I wasn't really trying to romance her anyway, so she could deal. We landed in a park, and once she'd gotten her bearings, she went to sit down on one of the benches with her head in her hands. I wasn't sure what to do, so I went and sat next to her.

"You shouldn't have bothered saving me," she said sadly, her voice slightly accented. "I'm a dead woman anyway."

"What did they want you for?"

"I tried to get out. But I know too much."

She was part of the Organization. The realization of what they probably did to people who tried to leave hit me hard in the gut.

"I can take you to the Legion." I tried to sound reassuring.

"And hide there forever?" She sighed. "I just wanted a normal life."

"But . . . aren't the Organization not supposed to interfere in people's personal lives?"

"Not supposed to." She shrugged. "But they make exceptions. I know about their Hounds."

"There's more than one?"

She nodded. "Martha had a protégé. She brought him over from Europe." She laughed and put her head into her hands again. "They're probably going to let him have me, when they catch me."

"They won't catch you," I said firmly. "I'm taking you to the Legion. You'll be safe there."

I took her to the Legion headquarters and filled out a whole incident report. It was weird being there so late too, and Captain Liberty showed up with his hair messy and wearing a sweater to talk quietly with the lady for a bit. Then as I was finally leaving to go home and sleep, he jogged up to me. "Blue, I need to speak with you."

I was kind of exhausted and annoyed, but I tried not to show it as I turned around. "Yeah?"

"You said that it was just a coincidence that you ran across the Organization kidnapping Miss Min. But she tells me that she was kidnapped by Jimmy Black."

"Uh." I shifted on my feet. "Yeah. Well, I didn't want to tell you."

"Why not?"

"I figured there wasn't anything you could do."

Captain Liberty shook his head. "Please never assume that, Blue. What happened?"

"Uh . . ." I took a deep breath. "He's been . . . you know, fighting the brainwashing again. He called me and told me what was going on, asked me to stop him."

Captain Liberty's eyes widened. "That was very brave of him."

"Yeah. Especially considering there's, like, nothing we can do for him. No, it's okay," I said as Captain Liberty opened his mouth to speak. "I get it. Don't want to start a war or anything."

"Blue. If Jimmy Black resigns voluntarily from the Organization, there's nothing they can do. We can protect him after that."

"But what if they go after him? Like they did with her." I gestured to the room where Miss Min was currently being interviewed.

"I can't promise that we can keep him out of the Organization's hands," said Captain Liberty. "But we can do our best. And that includes his family. Tell him that."

It was already starting to get light out by the time I crawled back through my bedroom window, relieved that my parents hadn't noticed I was gone. I stripped out of my costume, leaving it lying on the floor, and crawled into bed, shutting my eyes against the sunrise streaming through my window.

I couldn't sleep. I was thinking about Rick. Horrible things. I was worried they were torturing him, brainwashing him, making him hate me. Or worse, making him forget that he'd ever met me. If they found out what he'd done . . .

There was a knock on my window. My eyes flew open, and I sat up to see Rick crouched on the fire escape outside. I brought my hand to my mouth and stumbled toward him, tugging the window open and throwing myself into his arms, careless of the cold night air on my bare skin.

"Oh my god," I gasped. "I was so worried about you!"

He gave me a few quick kisses, and then climbed in through my window nervously. He looked pale and like he hadn't slept either, and an impressive bruise was forming on his chin where I'd probably hit him a bit too hard.

"They don't know anything yet," he said. "But I'm scared. What we did to Min . . . it's against code. The Legion wasn't supposed to know. They're angry at me. They don't suspect that I lost her on purpose, but if they start to . . ."

"Captain Liberty said that if you resign from the Organization, there's nothing they can do." I pulled him to my bed. He sat heavily next to me, still glancing around like we were going to be attacked at any second.

"Nothing they're supposed to do," he said quietly. "But they weren't supposed to go after Min either. They're not following the rules, don't you get it? They know who I am, they know who you are. Our families . . . We're not safe."

"They wouldn't risk antagonizing the Legion like that."

"I don't *know* what they would risk. Obviously I'm pretty valuable to them."

"Hey." I reached out to touch his cheek. "You're valuable to me too."

"I can't." He pulled away. "I'm all messed up in the head. I *want* to go back to them. I feel like I'm betraying my family."

"They're *not* your family," I said firmly.

"I know." He sounded frustrated. "But I feel like they are. I don't know, Javier. If I leave, there's no telling what they'll do to get me back. I mean, maybe I should just do the selfless thing and stay with them. Let them keep me like this."

I stared at him. "No!"

"You know it makes more sense. For my family, and for yours."

"I don't want to let you go, Rick. I won't." I stood and bent over him, touching my forehead to his. "Please don't tell me you really want me to."

Rick closed his eyes, his face strained. Then he grabbed my wrists and tugged me down for a kiss. I wrapped my arms around him, straddling him and kissing him hard. I was intensely aware of the fact that I wasn't wearing anything except my underwear. I wished we could be like this forever, with nothing to hide, nothing between us. I put everything into that kiss, hoping against hope that it would spark something in him, make him decide that I was worth fighting for. Eventually he pulled away, breathing heavily, and cradled my face in his hands. "I don't want you to let me go," he said roughly. "I want you to save me."

I nodded and got off him, rushing to pull on the first clothes I could find. Then I grabbed my phone and dialed the Legion's emergency number. "Hi," I said into the phone. "I need to talk to Captain Liberty right away."

Within half an hour, a bunch of Legion vehicles had shown up at our apartment to take us all to the headquarters. They'd been sent to Rick's family's house too. Rick had wanted to call and explain things to them, but Captain Liberty had warned him that it wasn't safe, because there was a good chance their phone lines were tapped. We waited anxiously in the Legion lobby until the cars drove up containing Rick's mom and dad, his sister, and their cat, as well as Kendall and her moms. I knew it was just a precaution, since the Organization probably wouldn't do anything to them, but I was still really relieved to see her.

Rick's parents were confused, of course, but Captain Liberty took them into a private room to discuss things with them. Apparently he was pretty used to having the *your child has superpowers* talk.

He came out a few minutes later, without Rick's family. "They'll be spending a few nights in one of our guest suites. How are you feeling, Rick?"

Rick's hand had been in mine the whole time, and he was incredibly fidgety, like I was the only thing holding him down. "You should lock me up," he muttered. "I—I'm fighting it, but it's hard." He gripped my hand really hard, and I pressed into him reassuringly. "Seriously, you need to get this out of my head. Now."

"We will," said the captain. "But first I need you to call the Organization, and tell them on record that you're resigning. Otherwise we'll be seen as having kidnapped you, which would break the truce we currently have. You understand?"

Rick swore. "Yes. All right, give me the phone."

"It's gonna be okay, Rick," I said, in the most reassuring voice I could manage, and he grabbed me and kissed the top of my head.

He dialed the Organization's number on his cell phone and turned on the speakerphone. His hand was so tight on mine, he'd probably have been breaking a normal person's bones. "Hello? This is Jimmy Black. I'm calling because . . . because I need to resign."

The guy on the other end sounded surprised, but pleasant. "Resign?" He paused. "I'm afraid that's not something you can do over the phone, Jimmy. You'd have to come in and do it in person."

"Why?"

"Well, for obvious reasons. One, we need to make certain that you aren't under duress. Secondly we have to check on the status of your family and friends, to make sure that they're not being held by the Legion as hostages in exchange for your loyalty."

"Damn it," said Captain Liberty quietly.

"Who said anything about the Legion?" Rick's voice was shaking. "I just don't want to do this anymore."

"Of course," said the man. "And we'll be happy to discuss that with you in person."

"Fine." Rick hung up and sat down heavily. "What the hell am I going to do now?" He looked at Captain Liberty. "Don't make me go back there."

"You can't," I said. "Captain, please."

"I'm not going to," said Captain Liberty. "I'm going to have to take this to the Legion council. But in the meantime, I'm going to have Chelsea remove your brainwashing. I'm certain no one will argue against that."

I breathed a sigh of relief that Rick echoed. Captain Liberty gestured for us to stand and follow him, and he tapped his phone to alert Chelsea that we were coming first. "We'll have to do it in the basement. Rick, you will probably have to be restrained."

Rick went white. I mean, he's always white, but you know. "Don't let me stop you. Whatever you do."

We went down into the horrible basement area, and Captain Liberty locked Rick in. I sat opposite the cell, waiting while he paced the room. "What if it doesn't work?" he said.

"I don't know. They managed to remove the brainwashing from everyone else."

"But what if . . . what if I'm not even brainwashed? What if this is just who I am?"

"Rick!"

There was a noise from behind us, and someone rushed in. "Vanessa!" Rick stepped up to the bars to meet her. "Oh my god. I missed you."

"I missed you too," said Vanessa. "The Raven had someone to meet." She glanced at me. "So they said I had to come here for protection. And then I saw Chelsea."

The door slid open, and Chelsea came in, looking determined.

"Can I stay with him?" I asked her.

She shook her head. "No. We need to be alone."

"Why?" asked Rick. "I want Javier here."

"I'm sorry," said Chelsea. "But you'll have to wait outside."

"It's okay." I took a few steps closer to the crackling red bars. "Rick, I'll be right outside. It'll all be over soon."

"What if I'm making a mistake?" Rick reached through the bars to grab my hand, his face twisted in fear. "Do you trust her?"

"I do," I said. "Please, Rick. Let her help you."

He closed his eyes, looking like he was trying to control his face. "Yeah. Okay. Please wait for me."

"Of course." I gave his hand a squeeze and then turned, my stomach doing somersaults, and left the room with Vanessa.

"I have some interesting news that will distract you," she said as we got into the elevator. "Did Ivana ever tell you she had a brother?"

I nodded. "I think so. A twin?"

"Yeah," said Vanessa. "Guess what? She found him."

I stared at her. "What?"

"Yeah, they spoke on the phone this morning! She was meeting him for lunch today."

"Wow." I blinked, surprised by the sudden good news. "That's awesome. They were separated, weren't they?"

"Yeah, like, forty years ago. It's really cool."

"What happened to him?"

"I don't know. I guess I'll find out tonight."

I'd thought it would maybe take a few minutes. But Vanessa and I sat by the elevator for hours. We talked a bit, but eventually she said that she had to go. "Tell him I'm sorry, I just can't handle being around people for more than a few hours at a time. I'll text you though."

"It's okay," I said. "I'm sure he'll understand." At that point it was hard to talk past the knots in my stomach anyway. Captain Liberty came by to see me, and explained that the council was voting overnight on what to do about Rick, but he was hopeful that they'd agree to protect him.

"They're good people," he said. "I'm confident they'll make the right decision. It's not just about Rick. The Organization cannot be allowed to get away with treating people this way. Something has to be done."

"He's been down there for hours," I said weakly.

Captain Liberty sat next to me on the bench. "Can I get you anything? A coffee?"

I shook my head. "How are my parents?"

"They're fine, I spoke to them on my way here."

"Okay." I nodded. "Does it usually take this long?"

"I imagine it's different for everyone." Captain Liberty looked at me sadly. "It'll be getting dark soon. Why don't you head to your room, and I'll call you as soon as it's done?"

I just shook my head again. "No. I'd rather wait here."

Captain Liberty nodded. "All right. But Rick will probably want to sleep afterward, and I'm certain he'll want to see his family."

"How are they taking it?"

He made a face that was almost a smile. "Well, his father had some choice things to say to me of the homophobic variety, but his mother and sister are just glad he's all right. His cat didn't seem too concerned either way."

I actually laughed. "Does his dad think we're, like, the Legion of Gay or what?"

"Well, that was apparently a serious concern when I first ran for the position of Captain Liberty. I'll stop by to check on you in a while." He winked at me and then stood up and walked off, leaving me gaping after him.

I pulled out my phone, and searched *captain justice gay* because I'm mature like that.

Dr. Paulo Flores, said the first result, *also known as Captain Liberty and previously Dr. Universe was married to Dr. Anna Ingles for eight years, and has been linked romantically with several male superheroes and other various key figures since and before then. Despite this, he has never publicly confirmed nor denied rumors of bisexuality, claiming that he wishes to keep his personal life private.*

I couldn't believe his superhero name was "Dr. Universe." I would never, ever have given up that name.

Someone else came by to check on me later, with an apology from Captain Liberty. Apparently he had to go oversee another meeting. And then I just sat there. I didn't need to be alone, really. Kendall could have come and waited with me, or my parents, or anyone. But I kind of selfishly wanted to be alone. When Rick got out, I wanted him all to myself. The last thing I wanted was for someone to show up and take him away from me.

Of course, that was exactly what happened.

When the elevator finally arrived, I stood, shoving my phone into my pocket and clenching my fists so hard that my nails dug into them. But instead of Rick, the doors slid open to reveal my parents, along with Rick's mom, and a tall beefy man with black hair and a strong nose that I assumed was Rick's dad.

I swear I almost threw up.

"Oh, Javier," said my mom in English. "We are just talking with Rick's parents."

"Mm-hmm." Rick's dad gave me a bona fide death glare. "How is he doing?"

"I don't know." My voice was wobbly. "I'm waiting for him to get out of treatment."

"I don't understand what they're doing with him." His mom seemed really scared. "It doesn't sound safe, or ethical."

"I don't . . ." I said. "I mean, they had to—"

"Don't worry about it, Javier," said my dad.

"I don't know who makes the decisions around here," said Rick's dad, and there was sweat trickling down his forehead. "But it seems like you were somehow involved." He took a step toward me. "And—"

"Excuse me." My mom moved between us. "I said to please not talk that way."

"Talk what way?" I felt incredibly uncomfortable.

"It's nothing." Rick's mom looked at her husband. "Right?"

"It certainly is something," said his dad angrily, "and just because these people don't want to take responsibility for their son's actions—"

Luckily at that moment the elevator dinged, and we all turned to stare as it opened to reveal Chelsea looking exhausted, and Rick behind her. He had an arm wrapped around himself, and was staring at the floor.

"Rick," I said softly. His eyes flicked up to me, all bloodshot and red-rimmed.

"Javier." His voice was hoarse. And then whatever he was going to say was cut off by his mom.

"Rick!" she gasped, running forward, and he let her hug him, looking relieved.

"Mom," he said. "You're here."

"Yes." She reached up to touch his face gently. "And Dad."

"Oh," said Rick, and he glanced at me as his dad embraced him awkwardly.

Rick was totally trying to get to me, but his dad was doing a fabulous job of getting in the way and making it look like a coincidence.

"We should get you to bed," he said, with a lot of false bravado, considering he'd been sweating and freaking out a minute ago. "Right, Miss . . ."

"Chelsea," said Chelsea dryly, and I could tell that she knew exactly what was going on. At least someone did. "Yes, it's probably best for him to rest."

"Right," said Rick's dad, and then they steered him away, and there was literally nothing I could do except watch them take him into the elevator and away from me.

I swear to god, I almost punched the wall. If my parents hadn't been there, I probably would have. Instead I collapsed back down onto the bench. My dad sat next to me while my mom stood and stared angrily at the elevator doors.

"Well," said my father. "Interesting family."

"It's not their fault." I sighed. "They were worried about Rick."

"Exactly," said my mom. "They should be worried about the danger their son is in, not that he is dating a boy. *Ay*, some people." She gave the elevator a nasty look and turned away.

"We can't all have great parents." I swallowed a lump in my throat.
"I really wanted to see him though."

"I know, *cariño*," said my dad. "You will."

I knew that I would see him eventually, but that just didn't seem good enough.

I was being selfish, but I couldn't help it. It seemed as if I'd been working for this for so long. To be alone with Rick, not even for any dirty reason. Just to kiss him, and talk with him, and make him feel comfortable. And now I couldn't even do that. And it was killing me.

CHAPTER SEVEN

"**O**ur absolute number one priority is the Hounds," said Captain Liberty.

We'd gathered together in his office for another private meeting. Part of me felt kind of special that I kept getting invited to all these important meetings, but I also felt awkward about it, and like I wanted to just go back to being a regular Junior Hero that wasn't involved with Hounds or the Organization.

Captain Liberty paced in front of his desk. "The Hounds are the reason the Organization is so confident, and they are the reason their numbers are so large. We absolutely must capture or otherwise remove them from the Organization's employ."

"So what do you suggest?" said the Wolfhound grumpily from his usual spot taking up half the couch. "We storm their HQ again? Do we even know where they relocated to?"

"We do," said Captain Liberty. "Miss Min was kind enough to supply us with that particular information. But the situation is undoubtedly delicate. Right now we have an uneasy truce with the Organization, and minimizing civilian casualties must remain of the utmost importance."

"Rick was a civilian until the Organization kidnapped him and did tests on him," I said bitterly, wishing that the Raven was here to back me up. She was still gone, I guess visiting her long-lost brother. I kind of felt like this was important enough for her to be here though.

"A fair point," said the captain. "We know that both Rick Rykov and Vanessa Larsen were victims of this. Who knows how many other civilians they've 'recruited' in this way, or for how long they've been doing it."

"The question," said Lady Deathquake, "isn't whether or not we should launch an attack on the Organization, but whether or not we have the resources to do so."

They'd been talking about this all morning, and it was frankly pretty boring after a while. I still hadn't gotten to go see Rick. I hadn't heard anything from him, or his family, and when I'd gone to see Captain Liberty about it, he'd just told me not to worry about it, and that there was a meeting he needed me present for. I was missing school today too, which was not great because Rick and I had been scheduled to present the oral part of our assignment today. I'd spoken to the teacher and gotten it switched to tomorrow, but I figured I'd probably have to do it by myself since Rick was apparently under family-enforced house arrest. He was probably snuggling with his cat right now instead of me. I didn't even like cats.

"We need to make a stand," said one of the other Heroes. "Our Junior Heroes shouldn't have to be afraid of the Organization kidnapping them or their families."

"Jimmy Black isn't one of our Junior Heroes," said the Wolfhound.

"He came to us for help," said Captain Liberty. "What the Organization did to him was inexcusable. If we let them have him back, we're no better than them."

"But if we choose to go to war against them," said Lady Deathquake. "Will we win again?"

Captain Liberty didn't think it was safe for me, Kendall, or Rick to go to school the next day. He showed up at my room that morning while I was getting ready to leave, and tried to convince me that he could just talk to my teacher and ask her to give me an exception on the project because of extenuating circumstances or whatever.

"Yeah," I said, hoisting my backpack over my shoulders. "No. I do not need Captain Liberty waltzing into my school to make excuses for my absences. Anyway, it's not like I'm a civilian. I can take care of myself."

He didn't look satisfied. "Javier, there's a lot going on right now. Everyone will understand if you don't feel like going to school. Your parents aren't going to work."

"Can I see Rick?"

"His parents don't want him seeing anyone," said Captain Liberty.

"You mean they don't want him seeing me."

"You understand that it's all I can do to keep them from up and leaving with him right now," he said patiently, and I sighed.

"Yeah, I know. But I really do need to do this presentation." At least I could help Rick get into college, even if I couldn't see him. "If anything happens, I promise I'll run away instead of getting into a fight." I gave him my biggest glow-y blue eyes. "Please?"

They must have worked, because he gave in, but he still insisted on driving me to school in his shiny black car, which wasn't conspicuous at all. And he told me he'd be back to pick me up after, so everyone was probably going to think I was involved with the mafia or whatever.

Anyway, I did my presentation no problem. I talked about the history of the city, and the Legion and the Organization, and what Captain Liberty had said about how the Legion tried their hardest to do the right thing. I think it was a pretty good presentation. I even made a few cheesy jokes. No one laughed. I was pretty sure if Rick had been there, he would have laughed. That didn't make me feel better, though.

Then, while I was sitting there listening to my classmates rehash every single historical point in Liberty City's existence over and over, my phone vibrated in my pocket. I glanced at the teacher, who was watching the presentation, and pulled it out under my desk. It was a text from a number I didn't recognize.

Javier. Its Rick. Help. Don't text back.

I stood up, my chair screeching, and rushed out of the classroom, my heart pounding. A couple of seconds later, another text arrived. *Raven. Hounds got her. She has vanessa. threatened my family i had to go with her.*

I called Captain Liberty, my hands shaking.

"Blue? I'm afraid I'm in a meeting right now."

"It's Rick! I think he's been kidnapped!"

There was a long pause, and a shuffling noise. "That's not possible, unless he's left the Legion."

"It's the Raven. The Hounds got to her. I don't know how. Maybe . . ." Her brother. Miss Min had mentioned that the Hound had brought over a protégé from Europe. Could that possibly have been . . . ?

More shuffling noises, and I realized that it was the captain running when I heard loud footsteps and a door opening. Then he swore, which would have been funny if it weren't for the circumstances. "This is definitely Ivana's handiwork. Goddamn it."

"Is his family all right?" I asked urgently, and he didn't answer for a few seconds—in which I had a mini-heart attack.

"Yes," he said finally. "They're alive. She wasn't gentle though. No sign of Rick."

I swore too, really loudly, and a teacher passing by gave me a grumpy look. "They can't get him back!" My voice went all stupid, like I was crying. "Please, you have to do something."

"Javier," said Captain Liberty calmly. "I need you back here at the Legion right away, do you understand? Do you want me to send someone to pick you up?"

"No." I swallowed hard several times. "I'll be right there."

I didn't even bother to tell anyone where I was going. I left the school at a run and hid in an alley, quickly changing into my costume so that I could run to the Legion. I made it to the building in record time, and Kendall met me in the lobby.

"Captain Liberty is on the roof," she said. "He wants you to meet him there."

"What's happening?" I asked as we ran to the elevator together.

"I don't know, exactly." She shook her head. "I think they're planning to attack the Organization though."

"I just want Rick to be all right," I said, my fists clenched.

"I know," she said cautiously. "But I want *you* to be all right, Javier. And so do your parents. Remember that, okay?"

"Yeah." My heart was pounding. "I'll be careful."

We emerged on the top floor in a huge hangar, the ceiling open to the sky, where no less than five Legion jets were buzzing with people getting them ready to fly. Captain Liberty was standing next to one, and he waved me over when he saw me.

"What's going on?" I jogged up to him. The ball of worry in the pit of my stomach made running feel weird.

"The investigation of the Organization headquarters finished early this morning." He reached out to grab a utility belt from someone and clipped it around his waist. He was wearing a much more modern suit than his regular retro spandex one, and he looked all business and kind of sexy. Ew, sorry. "Our sources confirmed that Rick Rykov and Vanessa Larsen have been captured by the Organization, and the council voted unanimously for an immediate strike on their headquarters. We've called for a civilian evacuation. As soon as it's completed, we will begin the strike."

"Okay," I actually sounded pretty calm considering I'd just been told we were, like, basically going to war. "Do we know anything about Rick?"

"He managed to grab his sister's cell phone before he was taken," said Captain Liberty. "Luckily it had geo-tracking enabled. We tracked it to the Organization before the transmission was cut off. Likely they discovered he had it and destroyed it."

I tried not to think about what they must have done with Rick when they found out about the tracker. And how badly had Ivana been brainwashed? "How long until the evacuation is done?"

"An hour. But we're heading there now." The ramp to the jet behind Captain Liberty opened, and he stepped up into it, gesturing me to follow. Lady Deathquake was waiting inside, along with several other heroes that I didn't know very well personally, but I recognized as being pretty darn famous. "We want to make sure they don't try to remove their prisoners to a secure location before we can get to them."

Flying in the jet was terrifying. Last time I'd been in it I hadn't really been paying attention, the time before that I'd been comatose from being stabbed, and the only time I'd flown in a regular plane was on the way to America, which I didn't remember much of. There were a lot of loud, worrying noises, and I couldn't help but remember that the floor was basically just a piece of metal with the sky underneath. Then we went into the cockpit, with its big windows looking out over the city, and I almost puked.

Not that it wasn't beautiful, seeing the hangar disappear under us, and then the city sprawling away beneath us as we flew. From what I could tell, we were heading toward the business sector again, but quite a ways south from where the original building had been.

"That's it." Captain Liberty pointed to a tall, squat building with a big silver spire on the roof. As we got closer, I could see that there was a helicopter sitting on the roof, with men in black surrounding it.

"Get close," Captain Liberty called to the pilot. "Stay out of firing range, and open the doors. Blue, Deathquake, with me."

We both followed him down into the belly of the jet, and the sides opened up, buffeting us in the face with wind and giving us a view of the roof. I could see the figures there moving, and then the door on the rooftop opened, and the Raven, Rick, Vanessa, and the old lady Hound all came out, flanked by men in black suits. There was also a smaller guy standing close to the Raven, who I bet was the second Hound, her brother. The Raven had Rick's arms locked behind his back, and one of the men in black was holding Vanessa while the other held a phone up to her.

Lady Deathquake put a hand up to her ear. "Sir. They're pressuring her to confess that she came of her own accord, so that you'll call off the attack."

"Get Williams on the line," said Captain Liberty. "Tell him that it won't happen, regardless of what they do to her."

The man holding the phone to Vanessa's ear lifted a gun and pointed it at Rick.

"No!" I lunged forward, but Captain Liberty put a hand on my shoulder.

"They have guns, it's not safe."

I turned to argue with him, and that's when I heard the shots. I felt like all the air had left my lungs, but when I looked, the two gunmen were on the ground, and Vanessa was staring down at them.

The Hound started screaming—I could hear her screechy voice all the way from the jet—and she pointed at Vanessa. The other Hound grabbed Vanessa's arms, and dragged them behind her back, and then Rick managed to pull away from the Raven long enough to hit her. They started fighting while the Hounds dragged Vanessa toward the helicopter. Then Rick took a kick to the gut, and the Raven slung him over her shoulder and ran toward the helicopter just as the blades started turning.

I had to look away as it started to rise, because the hot midday sun was directly behind the helicopter and it almost blinded me.

"Get closer," Captain Liberty was ordering the pilot. "Don't let them get airborne."

"Any closer and we'll be in firing range," said Lady Deathquake.

"Firing range of *what*?" I shouted.

"Our sources reported heavy artillery in the building's spire," said Captain Liberty. "If they hit the jet, we'll all go down."

"We have to do something," I said, as the helicopter continued to rise so that it was almost directly above the jet. "I'll go after them!"

"No!" said Captain Liberty. "I forbid you to go after them, Blue."

"I can do it! Kanaan can deflect bullets, right?"

"They can!" yelled Captain Liberty. "Doesn't mean they always do." He grabbed my arm. "Don't be stupid. We'll follow the helicopter to its destination."

"What if we lose them?" I shouted. "What if I never see him again?"

"Do you think I want to be the one to explain to your parents that I let you die?" he said angrily. "Do what I say!"

I pulled my arm away from him and jumped out the door.

It was way higher up than I'd ever been, and I only had my stupid fall-flying to keep me from dropping down to my death, but I couldn't think about that. I jumped up so that I was above the helicopter and then dropped, using my momentum and blasts from my feet to aim me toward the door. The pilot pulled out a gun and aimed it at me, and I almost freaked out. But then I brought my hands up and listened for the whistling of the bullet coming toward me, and deflected it with a sonic burst just in time.

Holy crap! Talk about adrenaline. The wind was roaring in my ears, and the light was making it hard to see, but somehow I managed to dodge two more bullets and deflect a third one before landing directly on the guy, ramming myself into him and knocking his gun out the window. It took a few seconds to orient myself on the floor of the helicopter, and then the Raven was lunging at me, grappling with me the best she could in the confined space.

I took a moment to reflect on how Captain Liberty was right, that I should have spent more time in the Legion gym training in hand-to-hand combat. But it was too late for that. The Raven wasn't pulling punches, smashing me hard in the kneecap, and then another in the stomach, all with a look of cold fury in her eyes that I didn't recognize at all. I saw stars, and she grabbed me by my neck, raising me up and forming a fist to knock me into tomorrow.

Then a metal pole smashed into the side of her head and she fell, her fingers slipping from my neck. Vanessa dropped the pole and stared at me, her eyes wide. For a second I thought it was all over, and then Martha attacked.

I probably would have been in a better position to fight her if I hadn't just gotten the snot kicked out of me by Ivana. For some reason the Hound lunging at me, screeching, her eyes all black and hollow, and her clawlike nails scratching at me made me want to just curl up into a ball and let her rip me to shreds. And then Rick leaped at her, scrabbling at her floral dress and wrapping his arms around her middle. She grabbed me though, her claws digging into the skin of my neck and her fingers like vise grips on my ears, and when Rick attempted to drag her off me, she pulled me after her, and then we were both flying out the side of the helicopter and falling.

I couldn't tell which way was up. The Hound's hands were on my ears, her big black eyes right in front of mine, and for a second I felt her dig into my head, making me forget everything, my powers, my family, Rick, the Legion. There was just falling, and hot, blaring sun, and emptiness, and then we landed heavily on the roof of the jet. I heard a bone crack, although I didn't know whose it was, and then the roof opened under us, and we fell again, landing on the black rubber floor.

There was a commotion, and I blinked, my vision blurry, to see a bunch of people scrambling around Martha, and someone stabbing her with a needle that made her collapse.

I stood and had just gotten my bearings when a huge explosion rocked the whole jet and sent me flying off my feet again. I nearly slid off the open edge of the jet, and just managed to grab hold of the side before I remembered that I wasn't actually in danger of falling to my death. It sure felt like I was.

The jet was heading down toward the building with the big spire. The spire itself had opened up to reveal several huge guns, which were shooting at us. Another one hit, and I decided that probably falling was going to be safer than hanging from an exploding plane, and let go accordingly.

I jumped down to the top of the building, and looked up to see the huge black hulk of the helicopter zooming down through the air toward me. I leaped again, barely getting out of the way in time, and it crashed into the roof with a horrible metal-scraping noise, tearing up the cement and metal as it slid toward the spire and collided with the base. As I landed, someone crawled out of the side of the helicopter. At that point I could probably have recognized that figure anywhere. It was Rick. He was okay, and he had Vanessa with him.

"Rick!" I yelled, waving at him, and then there was another horrible screeching noise, and I looked over to see the big metal weapons-of-death spire tilting, and breaking apart as it fell, the ruins of the helicopter directly in its path.

I screamed Rick's name and lunged forward. I went so fast that I couldn't see where I was going, but I collided with Rick's big rock-hard body, and wrapped my arm around Vanessa's delicate frame too, and then we all went flying. Rick seemed to realize what was happening in midair, and he turned so that we were on top of him. His back took the full impact of the cement as we landed and skidded out of the way. Just in time too, as the spire landed, crashing down on the helicopter's remains.

The whole thing exploded. The hot wind whipped my face, and I turned around to protect my eyes from the light and debris.

"Ivana!" screamed Vanessa, and my stomach dropped. Had she been in the helicopter?

I looked back as soon as the explosion died down, searching the debris for any sign of life. There was nothing but the hot crackling of the fire and the smell of gas and burning paint.

There was another explosion, and the building shook under us.

"We should get out of here," said Rick. "Come on."

We raced for the side of the building and looked down to see total chaos. The Legion jet had crashed into the base of the building next to us, leaving a giant swath of destruction in its wake, and a huge battle was going on. I mean serious. Captain Liberty was fighting with some guy with fires for hands, and Lady Deathquake was taking on a whole group of gunmen by herself.

"Oh no," said Vanessa. "Look."

She was pointing at the wreckage of the jet. If I squinted, I could just make out two figures. A man in a suit, and a little old woman—the Hound. She looked half-conscious, and the man was dragging her away from the fighting toward a black car.

"Javi," said Rick, his voice raspy, "if she gets away—"

I jumped off the building, and Rick started down the side with Vanessa on his back. He was pretty fast at running down the wall, but I was faster. I'd never done so much falling in my life, and I wasn't getting any fonder of it. I stopped myself just before hitting the ground, managing to only make a small crater this time, and bounded away toward the wreckage.

An unfortunate side effect of my powers is the noises I give off, and the man in the suit must have heard me coming from a mile away. When he turned, I recognized him as Williams, and a whole new level of rage surged up through me. Before I could properly channel that rage though, he pulled out a gun and shot at me.

I dodged, barely, deflecting the bullet but having to shoot myself off in the opposite direction in the process. I hit the side of the jet and fell to the ground, my head swimming. When I finally pulled myself up, there was no time to do anything besides watch as Williams slammed the car door and got into the front seat. I ran forward, but the car was already starting up, wheels screeching as it sped away from the battle.

Then something dark lunged in front of it, and the car hit it with a horrible crash. It's back wheels lifted up and the front fender wrapped around the obstacle.

I thought I heard Vanessa scream, but I wasn't thinking properly. I ran forward on foot, forgetting all about my powers, and shouted something unintelligible as Williams stepped out of the car, shutting the door behind him and walking around to the mutilated front. The wind picked up, and the smoke blew away a little to reveal Rick, his knees bent and his shoulder wedged into the front of the car. Williams grabbed him and yanked him forward, and Rick fell to his knees.

"Failed experiment." Williams aimed the gun at Rick's head.

"No!"

The gun went off, but the shot flew wide as Vanessa attached herself to Williams, yanking his head back and gouging at his eyes with her fingernails. Her eyes were black, and Williams's widened, full of horror, as if Vanessa was projecting some terrible image into his head. She wrestled the gun from him, and let him drop to the ground, where he cowered as she pointed the gun at his head.

"Vanessa," said Rick from where he'd fallen. "Stop."

"Yes, Vanessa," said a voice. "Stop."

It was the Hound. She had opened the car door, and had inched her way out from behind the deployed air bag. Rick's head whipped up, and he stared at her, his eyes glazing over.

"Rick!" I shouted.

Rick's eyes jumped to me. "Javier," he said slowly, reaching his hand up to touch the bloody mess that was his arm. "It hurts."

"Only for now," said the Hound sweetly. "Come to me, Rick. I'll make the pain go away."

"Don't touch him," spat Vanessa.

The Hound smiled at her. "You should know, my dear. I don't have to. Rick," she said again, her voice honeysuckle sweet. "Get rid of these nuisances, will you? Let's go away."

"Don't you dare." Vanessa's hands shook as they held the gun to Williams's head. "Rick."

"I . . ." Rick's eyes darted between her and the Hound. He seemed confused. I wanted desperately to go to him, but the Hound was in front of him, and I was afraid she would make him do something terrible if I did.

Then Williams moved, pulling a knife from his shoe and swiping at Vanessa's legs. Vanessa screamed and shot the gun, and for a moment I could swear time slowed down as the bullet raced toward his head. Then time stopped altogether, and Williams disappeared. When things went back to normal, it took me a moment to realize what had happened. Captain Liberty, of course. He had Williams, cuffing his hands behind his back, and he was standing between the Hound and Rick.

"Blue," said Captain Liberty. "Don't come any closer."

But it was too late. I'd already run toward them, and the Hound had turned to me, her eyes big and black and stretching across her face like she was a demon straight out of hell. She latched her fingers onto my face, and I swear she reached into my head and tore at every shred of confidence and happiness I'd ever felt, as if she could rip it right out of my skull. I was probably screaming, but I couldn't hear anything. And then, strangely, everything went purple.

The Hound's face was frozen in that horrible expression, her mouth wide, but then her claws slowly unhinged from my face, and she started to rise into the air. I gaped as she rose, higher and higher, her entire figure enclosed in a purple glow. Then the glow disappeared, and she dropped onto the rubble with a hideous cracking noise.

"That," said a voice with a familiar, razor-sharp accent, "was for my brother."

"He should have let me kill Williams," said Vanessa bitterly.

I sighed, and leaned my head against her. "You'd have regretted it."

We were waiting outside the Legion hospital wing, where we'd been for the last four hours, to hear of any news about Rick and Ivana. Ivana had managed to teleport out of the exploding helicopter, but had still been caught in the blast and sustained some pretty serious injuries. And Rick had, well, been hit by a car. Among other things. I was exhausted, and I wanted nothing more than to sleep, but Rick's parents were here too, looking pretty worse for wear, and damned if I was going to let them keep him away from me this time.

"I guess," said Vanessa noncommittally.

I looked up at her, worried, and she pulled a face at me.

"I'm kidding." She softened. "I don't really want to kill many more people if I can help it."

I snorted. It really wasn't funny, but I was overtired, and worried, and probably not in my right mind. "I suppose that's all we can hope for."

The door opened, and Kendall sneaked back in, holding three paper cups of coffee. Vanessa and I took them gratefully.

"Any news?" asked Kendall, and I shook my head. "Your parents said they can come down and wait with you if you want."

"It's okay." I sipped my coffee. "How's things on the outside?"

Kendall shrugged. "Not much to report. I mean, there is, judging by the amount of reporters outside, but you know." She rolled her eyes. "They're calling it a 'decisive victory.' The Organization is history. Apparently."

"Right," I said. "Well, that'll be good for public opinion. Captain Liberty'll be happy."

As if on cue, the hospital doors slid open, and Captain Liberty stepped out. He was still wearing his battle outfit, and his hair was all messy and sweaty from the fight, and if I hadn't been so worried about Rick, I probably would have, um, you know, *noticed*. As it was, I was only concerned about one thing.

Rick's mom beat me to it. "Is Rick going to be all right?"

Captain Liberty nodded. "He's got some pretty bad injuries, but he should have a full recovery."

"And Ivana?" asked Vanessa, and he nodded as well.

"Third-degree burns, and some mental scarring, according to Chelsea." He glanced back. "But, well, it's Ivana. She's had worse."

"Can we go and see Rick?" Rick's mom once again beat me to the punch, but Captain Liberty shook his head.

"He's resting right now, no visitors, under strict orders from the doctor."

"What?" said his mom angrily, and his father stepped forward. I could tell they were about to freak out at the captain, and they would probably eventually get their way, and well, I just didn't want to hear it. Obviously I wasn't going to get to see Rick again, not for ages. I turned to leave.

"You'll have to speak with the doctor," said Captain Liberty to Rick's parents, sidestepping them. "I'm just the messenger. Er, Javier, could I see you in the next room please?"

"Uh," I said. "Okay."

I followed him down the hallway and into an empty office, my stomach sinking. He closed the door and turned to me.

"Right," I said. "You're going to lecture me about how I disobeyed you, and could have been killed and stuff. Go ahead."

Captain Liberty looked surprised. "Not at all. I was just going to let you know that Rick is currently awake and alert, and they've left his window open so that he can get some fresh air."

I tilted my head at him, confused. "Okay, good?"

"And—" Captain Liberty walked over to the shiny floor-length window "—I believe this one opens too." He wrenched it open. "Yes, there you go."

I stared at him, excitement rising in my chest. "Are you serious?"

"Well," said Captain Liberty. "Suppose I ought to go and make my official statement to the press. Do you think I should change first?"

I shook my head, my face breaking into a grin. "No, I think you look great like that."

"Oh good." He gave me a little smile in return, and left.

I stepped up to the edge of the window, taking a moment to experience the thrill of vertigo from the ground being so very far away. Then I jumped out and shot myself to the nearest open window like a rocket.

I was pretty sure Captain Liberty had been telling the truth about the doctor not wanting Rick to have any visitors, so I made sure to be as silent as possible as I dropped to the floor in the hospital room.

Rick was lying in the bed. His arm and most of his right side were covered in bandages and casts, and his neck and part of his chin were shiny with burns. But his eyes lit up when he saw me, and he tried to get up.

"Don't." I rushed to sit next to him. "I'm not supposed to be in here."

"Thought you just liked coming in through the window," he said with a weak smile.

A big rush of relief welled up through me, and I stood and pressed my forehead to his. "Rick," I said, my voice breaking a little. "I was so worried about you. I just wanted to see you, and your parents were hogging you and I couldn't—"

"Javi." Rick reached up with his good arm and touched my face. "I'm sorry, I should have snuck off to see you earlier. I was scared."

"Of what?"

"I don't know." He shifted, and a little spasm of pain crossed his face. "I was worried you . . . hated me. All the bad stuff I did."

I kissed him, pressing my mouth to his, drinking in the feel of his lips and his warm body, and the exhilaration of him kissing me back. I kept kissing him until my back cramped and I had to straighten up a bit. "Does that alleviate your fears at all?"

He chuckled. "Yeah. A little." Then his face went serious. "Javi, what happened? The Hound . . ."

"They captured her," I said. "She's being kept somewhere where she can't hurt anyone else."

"What about the other one?"

I shook my head. "No one knows. Either he died in the helicopter crash or else he got away."

Rick frowned. "That's a problem."

"Yeah." I sighed and sat down. "Nothing can ever be simple, can it?"

"No," he said. "I guess that's a good thing." He gave me a big dopey smile. "At least I know how I feel about you, though."

"You're on drugs," I said, but I could feel myself smiling. My heart was going to freaking burst right there in the hospital room. Well, at least I had immediate access to medical aid.

"Yeah." Rick settled into the bed, looking sleepy and happy. "You should probably go before the doctor comes in."

"Probably," I said, but I didn't get up from the chair.

"Javi," said Rick, his face serious again. "I'll see you soon."

I took a deep breath. "It's just . . . your parents."

"I don't give a crap what my parents say," said Rick. "I'm going to see you soon. I promise."

I nodded. "Okay."

"Mr. Rykov?" said a voice outside the room. "Are you doing all right in there?"

"Fine," said Rick loudly, and then to me, "You should go."

He waved me on with his good hand. I stood and gave him one more lingering kiss, and then I went to the window, jumping up onto the windowsill and glancing back at him.

"See you soon, Blue Spark." He grinned.

I stuck my tongue out at him, and turned to look down at the ground, and then up at the city stretching away toward the setting sun. I swallowed down the fear whirling in my stomach, and gritted my teeth. Then I took a big deep breath, and jumped.

Dear Reader,

Thank you for reading J.K. Pendragon's *Junior Hero Blues*!

We know your time is precious and you have many, many entertainment options, so it means a lot that you've chosen to spend your time reading. We really hope you enjoyed it.

We'd be honored if you'd consider posting a review—good or bad—on sites like **Amazon, Barnes & Noble, Kobo, Goodreads, Twitter, Facebook, Tumblr,** and your blog or website. We'd also be honored if you told your friends and family about this book. Word of mouth is a book's lifeblood!

For more information on upcoming releases, author interviews, blog tours, contests, giveaways, and more, please sign up for our weekly, spam-free newsletter and visit us around the web:

Newsletter: tritonya.com/newsletter.php
Twitter: twitter.com/TritonBooks
Tumblr: tritonbooks.tumblr.com

Thank you so much for Reading the Rainbow!

Tritonya.com

TRITON BOOKS

AN IMPRINT OF RIPTIDE PUBLISHING.

ACKNOWLEDGMENTS

First and foremost, I have to thank my amazing partner Laurence, for indulging me when I said, "I want to come up with a story about superheroes!" and then hashing out the whole thing with me. Thank you also for letting me borrow Rick, even though he's technically your character. I hope I did him justice!

Secondly my awesome betas, Alex and Cara. Thank you for reading everything I send you. Your feedback always reassures me!

And finally the staff at Riptide, you have all been so welcoming and wonderful to work with. Particularly Sarah, you are incredible, and May and Alex, for the kickass editing job.

Having written this book, I can't help but feel like it's the kind of book I would have loved to have come across as a young confused queer teen. To that end, I hope that this book reaches some similar young (confused or not) queer teens, and that they find some joy in seeing a bit of themselves reflected in it. You are all superheroes!

also by
J·K· PENDRAGON

The Fairy Gift
The Gentleman and the Rogue
Prince of the Forgotten Planet
Ink & Flowers
To Summon Nightmares
Double Take (Part of *Geek Out: A Collection of Trans and Genderqueer Romance*)
Witch, Cat and Cobb
Sea Lover (coming 2017)

about
THE AUTHOR

J.K. Pendragon is a Canadian author with a love of all things romantic and fantastical. They first came to the queer fiction community through m/m romance, but soon began to branch off into writing other queer fiction as well. As a bisexual and genderqueer person, J.K. is dedicated to producing diverse, entertaining fiction that showcases characters across the rainbow spectrum, and provides queer characters with the happy endings they are so often denied.

After writing in the romance community for several years, *Junior Hero Blues* is J.K.'s first book for young adults. Having been very positively affected by the queer books they came across as a teen, J.K. hopes their young adult books can have a similar effect on teens who may have a harder time finding books about people like themselves.

Notable works by J.K. Pendragon include *Ink & Flowers*, a contemporary romance novel with coming-out themes, and *To Summon Nightmares*, a horror-fantasy that follows the journey of a young trans man into a world of magic and danger. *To Summon Nightmares* is the winner of the 2015 Rainbow Awards' Best Transgender Fiction award. J.K. also contributed to Less Than Three Press's *Geek Out: A Collection of Trans and Genderqueer Romance*.

J.K. currently resides in British Columbia, Canada, with a boyfriend, a cat, and a large collection of artisanal teas that they really need to get around to drinking.

Find J.K. online at www.jkpendragon.com
Email: jes.k.pendragon@gmail.com
Twitter: @JKPendragon

CPSIA information can be obtained
at www.ICGtesting.com
Printed in the USA
LVOW08s0457291216
519057LV00001B/112/P